ADVANCE PRAISE

Stigmatized, mischaracterized and misunderstood for generations; don't let those first impressions fool you! Turner will take you on an enriched cultural odyssey with one of the most misunderstood biblical characters. If asked about this character, you too might repeat what has been most rumored about her. This book is passionately written from a married woman's perspective, and the author turns everything you thought you knew upside down! She gives a 360 degree look into the culture and the life-changing encounters of a woman most noted as a "bad girl" that "woman at the well".

You will have hope again!

C.R.

BOOK PREFACE

Christians have for many years endured the "bad press" of being boring, unimaginative and taking things too seriously. Actually, I believe Christian creativity brings a breath of fresh air to an otherwise common existence. The truth of the matter is that there are creative and imaginative minds at work in Christendom. Such creativity may be purposed toward Art, Music, Dance and Literature- both fiction and non-fiction.

I have been blessed to read the work of Pastor Theresa Turner. This is a fascinating storyline that blends fantasy with fact. It has romance without getting sickeningly sentimental, and woven within the storyline; her message of hope comes alive.

The Saints will be encouraged and the Unsaved will be curious. Her approach to the subject matter speaks to the tradition of a C.S. Lewis novel.

Enjoy the read!
Apostle Kevin E. Dean

LAMARRA

THE WOMAN AT THE WELL

Theresa Bean Turner

Chicago, Illinois

November Media Publishing, Chicago IL.
Copyright © 2017 Theresa Bean Turner

November Media
info@novembermediapublishing.com

Ordering Information: Special discounts are available on quantity purchases by corporations, associations, and others. For details, contact the publisher at the email address above.
Printed in the United States of America

Produced & Published By November Media Publishing
ISBN: 978-0-9990431-7-2

Adapted from the play: The Woman at the Well copyright 2008
Scripture references: KJV Bible and Gods Word Versions

First Edition : November 2017

10 9 8 7 6 5 4 3 2 1

DEDICATION

This book is dedicated to my family and friends who encouraged me to complete this work that was given to me by our Lord Jesus Christ.

"The thing that hath been, it is that which shall be; and that which is done is that which shall be done: and there is no new thing under the sun."
Ecclesiastes 1:9 KJV

The Preacher - King Solomon

CHAPTER ONE

"Is he dead? Is he dead? What are you saying? Is he dead?"

"God, oh no, not again. Not my love." She felt her heart ripping out of her chest.

She awakened, screaming in a cold sweat. "How many times must I relive this nightmare," she thought as she rolled out of her cold, wet bed, to escape her tortured sleep.

Relieved to be starting another day, she got dressed, did a few chores around her home, and prepared to head to the well so that she could get water for her meal that afternoon.

As she walked down the path, the sun was bearing down on her with a great unyielding presence just like the dream she had last night. The oppressive rays were not as harmful as the continuous assault Lamarra was subject to everyday at the well, but today would be different.

"I will not respond to their remarks," she told herself. "I'll go get my water and say nothing to no one." She strengthened herself for the possible attacks. Her thick skin had grown thinner with each encounter, but she made her way to the well, where her tormentors had gathered.

The portly woman said "I don't have any lentils for my meal tonight. So, I sent my daughter to my mother-in-law to get some. I hope she doesn't stay too long listening to those old stories mother tells all the time. There is much to do, and I need her help!"

The skinny woman responded, "Your daughter is obedient and very smart. She will return soon." As she turned to look for her daughter, she saw someone approach. "Here comes Ariel. I don't know why she comes to the well when she has handmaids to do that for her."

The portly woman said, "She just wants us to see her finery and make us feel little in our own eyes." Ariel and her handmaiden approached the well.

Ariel broke the ice first. "Good morning, my sisters. God's blessings to you. What a beautiful day the Lord has made. Let's rejoice and be glad in it!"

The skinny woman said, "I guess you can rejoice. You're blessed to have handmaids to help you. Is she new to the household?"

"No," Ariel said without missing the insinuation of a second wife, "You just haven't seen her before."

The portly woman said, "You amaze me, Ariel. You still watch over your handmaiden even when they draw your water. Don't you trust those that labor among you, or are you keeping them away from someone else?" Her sarcasm wasn't lost on Ariel.

"Jethro is already out with the sheep. I came to talk to you ladies."

The skinny lady said, "Well good thing your husband is gone because here comes Lamarra. She has an evil spirit on her, and every man she meets dies when they marry her." They huddled together as Ariel looked around.

The portly woman piped in, "I hear she has a new bed warmer, but does anyone remember a wedding feast?" The women hurried to collect their water.

Ariel walked over to Lamarra who was approaching them cautiously. "Good morning Lamarra. It's good to see you, since I haven't seen much of you lately. Have you been sick or something?" Ariel says as she backed away from her in case she did have some contagious disease.

Lamarra rolled her eyes at the other women and mumbled under her breathe, "Those nosy vultures."

Giving her attention to Ariel, "Hello Ariel. I've been busy, that's all."

The Portly woman retorted, "Does someone have you tied up all day?"

"Hmmm, you know he needs his rest sometimes, Lamarra."

Angrily, Lamarra responded, "If I were you, I'd stay out of my affairs and mind your own business, seeing that your husband left your house with a bundle of clothes. You better take care of your own house instead of meddling in mine." The portly woman scurried away making excuses. Lamarra was ready for a fight.

Ariel tried to calm her down by telling her "Ignore these silly women. She goads people just to get something to gossip about. She's been walking on eggshells lately; her husband has been mean to her and she's afraid."

Lamarra sighed, "I know how that feels. My third husband treated me the same way. I did everything I could to please him, but it wasn't enough. Then one day he came home with a bill of divorce. He said I hadn't been a good wife."

"Third husband?" Ariel said, "You told me about your first husband who you loved so much. You all were rarely seen by anyone."

Lamarra laughed as her eyes sparkled. "Oh yes, we obeyed the law." she giggled. "I love that the law requires that a man take a year off to make his wife happy, [1]and he did! I was so scared but, my mother said 'trust Jediah. He loves you, and he will be tender and loving towards you.' And he was. He

---

[1] Deuteronomy 24:5

always brought me something to remind me of him. The law is correct, that two became one [2]; where one was, you saw the other. Then, after a year, we were at war with the Assyrians and Jediah fell in battle. I was heartbroken. I didn't want to go on living without him."

Ariel's eyes teared up. "I can't image your husband dying and leaving you all alone!"

Lamarra told her, "My parents thought it best if I married Jediah's brother, Rehum, after the days of mourning [3]. It was to help us both recover from our loss, but that wasn't so. Rehum loved another just as I did, but he had not asked for her yet. The law says we could have a child to raise up to honor Jediah [4]. The priest and scribes thought it best," Lamarra said with a sad look in her eyes.

"It was good that you were taken care of instead of going back to your father's house to live!" Ariel said. Lamarra looked at her shaking her head.

---

[2] Genesis 2:24
[3] 1Samuel 31:13
[4] Deuteronomy 25:5
Jediah means Jehovah knows

"Ariel, you don't understand, Jediah was in every part of me. When we were together, even our breathing was the same pace. I loved him greatly and I couldn't give my heart to Rehum. I tried and so did he, but we both were miserable. We both loved other people. It was horrible. He was in the fields and was bitten by a viper and died. His parents treated me like an evil amulet around their neck that brought destruction to their home. I went back to my father's house and he treated me as if it were my fault. Abba was anxious for me to marry and have children. So, when he met a merchant in Samaria who inquired if I was married, he discussed a bride's price quickly. Abba thought it was best for me because the Merchant could take care of me. We moved to Joppa and I helped sell his merchandise. I didn't love him. I wasn't even attracted to him. He liked the way I looked, and he wanted children."

Ariel said, "But you could learn to love him. Over time, we see what our parents saw in them. They know what it takes for a marriage to survive."

Lamarra retorted bitterly, "For us to survive, to lose the person you love, marry the next person, and to try and go on as if they didn't exist! Submitting to a husband who considers you a cook, baby maker, and to exercise his husbandly rights. His thoughts for your welfare are third in the order of things. So, to actually be loved and important to him as a person and not an asset or a means to an end is miraculous. We subject ourselves so we don't have to sell our bodies on the streets for food and burden our families. Gad was truly a merchant. All he cared about was making money. Selling his wares and feeding his pride was his true love. When I didn't get pregnant after a year of marriage, he started calling me used goods and concluded I must be barren. He would go away on trips for a few days, frequently. Next thing I knew, he brought home a second wife, 14 years old and scared to death. He didn't want me around her. He was afraid my barrenness might rub off. He kept her very close to him. I rarely had a conversation with either one of them and definitely not with her. Yep, two months later she was throwing up all over the place. She didn't want my help or comfort in any way, as if I would harm her. Gad was mean to me and treated me like I was their slave. I never thought he would divorce me before she had the baby because she would need my help and support. I was willing to help her, but she didn't want my help; she wanted my position, as first wife! So, to please his young and conniving wife, he divorced me and kicked me out when she was seven months pregnant. I didn't want to go back home. I didn't want to see the look in my father's eyes and listen to how I needed to repent for my sins, ask forgiveness, and make a sin offering. I didn't want to hear how I couldn't keep a husband, that the Scribe's daughter was barren and even worse, unwanted. I didn't want to see the disappointment in mom's eyes of me not being a good wife. I couldn't face them or face who I had become. One of the widows in town let me stay with her so she would have a helping hand. Then, the widow told me that one of the merchants was looking for me to help him sell his wares. When I went to the market place to find him, it was Ezra, one of the richest merchants in Joppa. He had one of the largest booths, and he always had exotic items and beautiful clothing. He was the beginning of my nightmare."

Ariel was excited. "Joppa! I hear it's an exciting town with the ships and merchants coming and going. With all the foreign wares and merchandise in the markets, I hear it is one of the best! I heard that King Solomon brought all his timber and things to build the temple through that port. Is that where you met your present um... umm... husband?"

Lamarra ignored the question. "I lived there with my third and fourth husband. It was a nightmare for me. I can't talk about that now Ariel I have a lot to do today, I have to go, he will be looking for me. Be blessed," she said counting her fingers as she walked away. Lamarra was fussing at herself, "Why do you get into these useless conversations? Nothing is going to change. Men can still do what they want and treat us like dirt and throw us away. Lord, where are you? You know everything, and you can help us with everything. When are you coming to change this world? Messiah we need you... I need you now! We are surrounded by people that hate us. The Jews hate us, and they are our brothers. Lord, I have so many questions. Why can't we help and love one another?" She took the water in the house and filled the jars. Thank God! The house was empty, and she was alone for now. This was not the life she envisioned for herself. "Lord hear my prayers. I want everything you promised us: a prosperous life. I am willing and being obedient to what you have told me to do."

She went to the marketplace to get food for the evening meal. Men stared at her and whispered when she came around. They didn't like her handling the wares and food items. They almost treated her like a leper- unclean. The marketplace was filled with people. The traders were busy laying out their wares, children were playing in the streets, and lines were strung up with beautiful colored clothes and wares hanging and blowing in the breeze. She had a love-hate relationship with the marketplace. Some of her fondest and most painful memories were there. The beautiful clothing, vibrant colors, scented oils and the sights and sounds made it exciting. Meeting people from faraway places and hearing the news of what was going on in the world. Like, the news that there was one in the wilderness baptizing people and telling them to repent and turn to God, so they can be forgiven. Then there was the one about the Messiah, who would deliver a fatal blow to the head of the serpent[5]. Occasionally, she would see a trader or merchant that she knew in Joppa[6] who would be excited to see her and had heard of Ezra's unfortunate death. They were very kind to her and reminded her that God would help her; scarce words came from her neighbors. The only words she heard were whispered behind her back about her fall into sin. Her fathers named was mocked, that he taught everyone else's child but his own about sin. How dare they! They didn't know her or her situation. They had already judged her as guilty. If they could, they would carry out the sentence[7]. But mercy and grace abounded that there were those, no matter how few, who showed kindness and love. She was isolated in her own community. A few weeks later, she arose early in an attempt to arrive first at the well. Unfortunately, everyone had the same idea, and that was, to avoid

---

[5] Genesis 3:15
[6] Joppa means beautiful
[7] Genesis 38:24 -Tamar

Lamarra. She braced herself for a fight. This would be the last time she would be provoked by the wicked women at the well.

As they huddled together to weave their webs, one woman said, "Hurry and get our water so it doesn't become unclean from her using her it. If she touches it, you can become unclean too!" The skinny woman said.

"Be careful of her, whatever curse is on her you can take it back to your husbands and they will die because of her! Her latest buyer must not be aware how high a price he will pay." The portly woman said, "The price must be cheap to keep him deceived, so he's sticking around." Lamarra could not hold her peace, she was furious at them. How dare they talk about her like that! She had kept the law all her life. Now she had to put up with the serpent tongued women at the well. She threw her water on them and stormed off running into Ariel along the way.

Ariel stopped her. "Lamarra, are you cleaning the women with their clothes on? Don't give them the pleasure of upsetting you. They're trying to run you away. Don't give them the satisfaction!"

Lamarra shook her head and cried. "Ariel, I'm tired of taking abuse from everyone! I left Joppa and all that abuse behind for a new life in Sychar, and it's just a horse of another color!"

Ariel, still excited about Joppa, said "How could you leave beautiful Joppa for Sychar? There is no comparison. Life must have been pretty bad!" Tears welled up in Lamarra's eyes as she explained, "It was a living hell! After my fourth husband died, I asked God to help me to leave that place and come back to Sychar, His timing was perfect. One of my former customers was traveling north and allowed me to travel with them. It was truly a blessing.

With a puzzled look, Ariel asked, "wait a minute, your fourth husband died, what happened to him?"

Lamarra bristled, "I'm not going to rehash that history. Let's just say God knew what I needed, and he delivered. The day I left Joppa, I went to the market to get some provisions. I had made up my mind to take my chances on the road. It had to be better than living in Joppa. As I shopped, I saw one of my former customers and he recognized me. When I told him where I was going, he volunteered to escort me and assured me that he and his men wouldn't harm me."

"I must get back now Lamarra, I'll see you later." Ariel said as she walked away counting her fingers to remember how many husbands Lamarra had.

"All right, see you later." Lamarra waved goodbye.

CHAPTER TWO

Lamarra remembered the first time she saw Manni in the marketplace of Joppa. He had asked her to pick out something for his wife and to spare no expense! He was excited and couldn't wait to get home and see the look on his wife's face. She had seen him several times since then, but the last time she went to the well, she saw him leaning against a tree looking for someone. As he turned to survey the area, his eyes fell on Lamarra. He looked pleasantly surprised, and immediately went over to speak to her. She thought about how he had changed since that first day. He inquired about her and her husband's health and she told him of his demise.

Manni said "I saw another person at your booth and wondered where you two were. I'm so sorry for your loss. You all had very nice wares. When did he die?" He asked.

Lamarra said reluctantly, "He died last year and now I'm going back to my father's house in Samaria."

"Who is traveling with you?" he asked.

"I'm going alone because I have no relatives here and there is no one I know who is headed in that direction!" She said. Manni knew that was unwise, especially for a beautiful woman like Lamarra.

He could see she was determined to go, so he said, "Well if you don't mind traveling with some sheep herders and eating Obadiah's food, you can travel with us because we are headed north. I promise you will be safe. By the way, my name is Manehillel[8], but they call me Manni."

---

[8] Manni- means causing to forget.
Maneh- means a weight as in mina.
Hillel – means singing praising.

She responded, "My name is Lamarra, nice to finally meet you." Manni heard his men approaching and told her to meet him back here at the well. They would water the sheep and goats and then head out. She agreed and went to get her things from the widow's house. They said their goodbyes and prayed for one another. The old woman went to a small box on her shelf and pulled out a coin.

She told Lamarra "This coin is the last one from my bridal veil. I give it to you as a blessing for your marriage that it will be prosperous and joyful. That God will give you houses with good things you didn't fill, wells dug that you didn't dig, vineyards and olive trees which you didn't plant[9]. Remember, don't forget the LORD and what he has done for you!"

Lamarra hugged her and said, "I will never forget you and your kindness toward me. When everyone else forsook me, you took me in. Thank you, mother. I love you and will miss your love and wisdom."

---

[9] Deuteronomy 6:10-13

The widow said, "I have seen that man many times here in Joppa. He's well known and respected. You will be safe with him. Now, don't keep the man waiting and don't forget an old woman, remember me in your prayers." She gave the old widow a hug and a kiss and went to the well. Manni and his men were watering the sheep. He turned around as she approached and looked her up and down. She felt self-conscious and pulled her veil closer. He walked over to her and asked if she had additional belongings that she wanted to bring so they could help her carry them.

Lamarra said "This is all I have in my possession, a bundle and the clothes on my back." Manni was shocked; a merchant that rich and he leaves his wife looking like a beggar on the street. Her veil was practically transparent. It was so worn, that small bundle could hold only a few items. He realized she was self-conscious, so he gave her a few instructions. First, that she should stay close to him because he always wanted to insure her safety. Second, the men answered to him and have their instruction to leave her alone unless she specifically asks for their help when he's not around. Lastly, they would stop to rest a few times during the day and rest at night with an early rise every morning. Manni threw her bundle on one of the mules. He went back to the well and gave the men instructions and headed out talking to Lamarra. She talked about seeing him in the market place, and how he always seemed to be waiting or looking for someone. She inquired if he had family in Joppa.

Manni told her "My wife and I lived in Joppa for some time and made some very good friends. Whenever I'm in town I try to catch up with everyone. I meet a lot of people wherever I go and there are some people who leave a lasting impression on me. Those people I always hope to see again, like you!" She was surprised at her inclusion.

"How could I have impressed you, a well-traveled man of the world?" She laughed at herself. They shared stories about people they both knew in Joppa and their escapades. They talked all morning into the afternoon. Lamarra opened her water skin; it had its own cup attached to it. He wondered where that skin was made and how many she had sold. She offered everyone a drink from it. Manni had bread that he shared with everyone. Manni introduced Lamarra to the men as they sat and ate. Some of them were well-seasoned shepherds and a few of them were new at it. It was easy to discern the difference. They continued pressing on, so they could reach a nice area to put the sheep down for the night. As the sun began to set, everyone was busy settling down for the night. Manni had one of the men catch a bird for Obadiah to cook for them. Lamarra said she would love to cook it for them, he quickly agreed. She told him she was going into the bushes to relieve herself.

He told her, "I'm coming with you, but I will give you your privacy."

Lamarra said, "If you must." He stood watch facing the men, but in ear shot of her. He was very respectful and attentive. She felt strangely comfortable around Manni; he always put her at ease. He was very careful to tell her everything he was doing, but he had this intense look about him. He always looked her in the eye, all the way to her soul. He was very direct in his gaze and didn't shy away. One of the men remarked about him covering Lamarra, and he got angry! The man found himself on second watch for the remark. Lamarra tried to defuse the situation by busying herself preparing some food. She had picked a few spices and roots on the way. She saw some spices to pick and Manni followed along with her. He was still smoldering from the remark. Lamarra began to sing a song as she worked, and it stopped Manni dead in his tracks. She was singing the same song his mother would sing to him when he was upset. It would calm him down and soothe his hurts. He stood frozen in time, engulfed in the melody. The sweetness of her voice melted his heart and catapulted him back to his head on his mother's breast as she wiped away his tears.

"Everything will be just fine." She would say, "You are blessed of God and He loves you. You will be a man of greatness." His mother was his greatest source of encouragement. She loved him dearly, and he was her only son, protector and helper. Lamarra saw that he was far away in his peaceful memories. He hadn't thought of his mother in months. They walked back to the camp and

Lamarra took spices out of her satchel and began to grind them up. The man came back with the bird and she was quick to dress it and clean it. She rubbed the seasonings on with oil and put it over the fire. The aroma swirled through the camp and through Manni's memories of his mother's cooking. His mouth watered, and he looked over to Lamarra watching him. There was a hint of a smile on her face with softened eyes. He suddenly became self-conscious and pulled himself together as she observed his every move. He complimented her on the wonderful aroma that made him even hungrier.

She said, "I enjoy trying new spices as I travel because I can pull them fresh out of the ground."

Manni replied, "You wiggle your nose when you smell the leaves and then look to the side as if you're wondering what the aroma is."

"How do you know all that?" She asked, surprised that he noticed those things.

He said, "I've seen you in the marketplace buying your food, and may I say you are a good haggler. You get rock bottom prices," he laughed.

Lamarra pretended to be surprised and defended herself. "I've learned from the best of them. They came to my booth and tried to get gold for a denarius, and we would haggle all day until I got a decent price."

"They were dealing with a wily woman for sure. They couldn't get anything over on you!" Manni laughed. She made a muscle with her arm and her laughter filled the camp. Manni thought he would lose his mind because her laugh was intoxicating.

She touched his arm and asked, "Are you well? You don't look steady."

He looked at her brown eyes and smiled, and he said huskily, "I'm starving, and that roasted fowl smells delicious." Everything she did was larger than life. Her touch was soft and lingered slightly leaving him marked forever. He looked in her eyes and got lost in the amber flecks caught in the firelight. She was drawn by his gaze and had to tear herself away.

"Well, let me feed you before you faint," she said, rising to serve the men. Manni gestured to the others to come and eat. She served everyone first and then sat and ate herself. The lentils were great with the roasted fowl and herbs she gathered. The men were complimenting her food and one of them said even their wife's food wasn't this good at home, let alone on the road! They all laughed and were full, great food and decent company. Obadiah was glad not to cook and to enjoy this reprieve. He asked Lamarra to sing that song she was humming earlier. She sang it robustly and all the men applauded. Manni walked away.

She asked, "Did I do something wrong?"

Obadiah said, "No, he's just moody like that. Just give him some room, and he'll come around." Manni couldn't take it; she was like his mother in so many ways. It was tearing him up inside. He didn't want her to see him cry. Is it possible to be happy and sad at the same time?

He prayed, "God' why did you send this woman my way? She stirs up every memory that I had buried. She has exposed every tender area of my heart. WHY, TO TORTURE ME? Help me Lord to understand. She is remarkable but also mourning a dead husband. What will her father think about me escorting her home, a mere shepherd?" He saw Lamarra walking away from the camp with some containers. He followed her. She bent down to clean the pots, and he just stood over her, amazed. When she stood up and turned around, she was practically in his chest.

She stumbled backward saying, "Oh, I'm sorry." Manni didn't give her any room.

He was staring into her eyes [10]when he said, "You should be careful not to go off by yourself. Wild animals or thieves could be about. It's not safe for you." Shifting his conversation, he continued, "Thank you for a great meal, the men enjoyed it too. You amaze me. The food brought back so many memories of home. You're a good cook!"

Lamarra staring back at him said, "I enjoy cooking and watching people enjoy the food. Eating together is a great time for sharing and talking." The men were clearing the camp and settling in for the night. The men were on one side of the fire and Lamarra and Manni on the other side, with Manni positioning himself on the outer perimeter. He added more wood to the fire and talked for hours about the marketplace. They

---

[10] Song of Solomon 4:9

talked about the people they met, the cultural differences and languages they learned. Manni spoke 4 languages and 2 dialects. He loved the exotic things and shared some of his cultural mishaps to the roar of laughter from his men. She was excited to hear about the other lands, foods, and customs. She wanted to go there and see for herself now. He saw the excitement in her eyes and continued to talk just to have her full attention to himself. The men slowly bedded down for the night, bored with the old stories. Some of them were there and added their remarks. Lamarra cried with laughter about how they teased Manni. All he knew was that he was drunk on Lamarra. He talked incessantly, surprising himself. He hadn't said over two words to a woman in years, but tonight it flowed out so easily. It was fun and light hearted, and he felt free to enjoy life. Lamarra could not believe a man could out talk her, but here he was going on and on. His men were having a good time laughing at him, entertaining Lamarra. They had never seen him so… sociable. The brooding scowl was gone; he was a different person in her presence. Her eyes closed slowly and opened to his soothing voice that spoke to her soul. She struggled to keep them open.

He lulled her to sleep by slowly calling her name, "Lamarrrrra." It sounded like heaven calling. She opened her eyes and he was right in front of her apologizing.

"I have bored you to sleep with my stories. Go lie down and get some rest, we leave in the morning." Those sleepy smoky brown eyes[11] looked at him with loving tenderness. She apologized for falling asleep and made him promise to continue tomorrow. Later that night she dreamed she was in a faraway place with aromatic spices, beautiful fabrics, and a man's hand holding hers loosely but securely. He had rings on his hand, but she couldn't see what they were. She couldn't see his face, but she recognized he had a strong arm and solid torso. Who was this man? She awoke, startled at her thoughts and sat up breathing heavily with her chest heaving.

Manni spoke quietly to her, "Lamarra, are you alright?" It touched her very heart, the care and

---

[11] Proverbs 6:25

compassion in his voice. He was sincere about her welfare.

"I had a dream," she said, but she couldn't look at him.

"It must be very hard on you with your husband dying. The loss you must feel!" He responded. She was so embarrassed, she hadn't thought about her husband at all today. Guilt washed over her, and she bolted from her bedding, crying and sobbing into the surrounding darkness. Manni grabbed a branch from the fire and ran after her. One of the men got up to follow and Manni told him to stay at camp. He hesitated but stood his ground because he knew better!

"Lamarra! Where are you going? Stop running, it's dark you can't see." Shame and guilt flooded her mind as the tears flooded her eyes. She couldn't see a thing.

"What am I doing dreaming about this man? These new feelings I have about Manni ...a married man! Like you don't have enough problems. Another accusation and you're dead[12]! Girl, if you don't pull yourself together! What does

---

[12] Deuteronomy 22:22

that dream mean? Whose hand was that?" Just then she tripped on a tree limb and fell face first in the dirt. Manni came to her aid.

"Are you hurt?" he asked. "Can you walk? You hit your head and you're bleeding! Lamarra, what is wrong with you? You can't run off into the dark like that." He cleaned her cut with her veil as he brushed leaves and debris out of her hair and cleaned her wound by the light of the fire on the stick. Her eyes glistened with tears, and his heart went out to her.

He gently dabbed at the wound and softly inquired, "Are you hurt anywhere, Lamarra? Tell me so I can help you!" She hadn't known such tenderness since Jediah.

She was trying to assess her condition when one of the men came up and said, "Are you ok, ma'am?"

Before he could get the sentence out of his mouth, Manni whirled around and said through gritted teeth "Didn't I tell you to stay at the camp? Leave us alone, he growled." The man backed off reluctantly. Lamarra wrapped her mantle around her, but it caught fire from the flame. She dropped it, and it burned up in a flash. She started to run back to camp embarrassed and ashamed, but Manni grabbed her arm and pulled her alongside of him.

He was very stern with her when he said, "Slow down before you kill yourself. Walk in the light of the fire on the branch." She walked with him and was angry with herself for acting so foolishly.

"Who is he to speak to me as if I were his wife or something?" She snatched her arm away and said, "I can walk on my own!"

"You couldn't prove that to me a few minutes ago when you were on your face!" He retorted. "You ingrate," he mumbled under his breath.

Manni walked over to the other man and spoke harshly to him and said, "Why is it every time I tell you to do something, you do what you want to do? If you can't follow orders, you can find work with someone else. What I say is for the good of all of us."

The man defended himself, "I wanted to make sure she was safe and make sure that you didn't need my help."

Manni raised his brow and said, "We did need your help guarding the camp! I think I can handle a little woman on my own. Do what I tell you to do or there won't be a next time!! Do you understand?"

The man said, "Yes sir, I understand." He turned and asked "Lamarra, are you alright? Can I get you anything?"

Manni was trying to stay calm. "She's fine now go to your …"

Lamarra interjected, "I can speak for myself. Thank you for your concern, I am fine, except for my bruised pride." She gave him a little smile and he was satisfied and walked away. Manni was back to brooding and pacing as he watched their exchange. The man was a little sweet on Lamarra. He was always running around her like a little puppy dog trying to get her attention. He was annoying!!!! They all bedded down for the night with their thoughts and dreams.

CHAPTER THREE

It was a beautiful sunrise, and the air was cool and crisp. Manni loved his quiet time in the morning. He had the early morning watch to get everyone up and moving, which he did, after he had his time of prayer. Then he went out to survey the road they would take. Truly, this trip was divinely orchestrated. God had shown him areas in his life that needed to be healed. One woman made all this clear to him. He prayed for her that morning, that God would prosper and keep her and her family safe. When he returned to camp the aroma of food filled the air, and Lamarra was up waiting with breakfast. She sized him up as he approached her. He felt off balance around her. She had no problem confronting him or his ways. Nevertheless, he enjoyed her presence. Talking to her was easy and comfortable. He has known of her for years in the marketplace as someone else's wife. Now, he saw why she was married: she was captivating in every way. He put his guard up as he approached her fireside.

She studied his handsome face, and his expression seemed pensive. He walked with strength and ease in each stride. His torso was solid and accustomed to physical work. He didn't look like a shepherd out here in the hills. His clothing was custom fit and clean. His dark curly hair peaked out around his skullcap and framed his bronze face[13].

She said, "Good morning, Manni." He couldn't look at her because he felt exposed in her eyes and could not hide.

He pointed to the sky and said, "Another beautiful day the Lord has given us. Did you sleep well, Lamarra?"

---

[13] Song of Solomon 5:10-16

"My bruises didn't keep me awake, if that's what you're asking." she quipped. He refused to argue with her because she and the day were too beautiful to miss!

He took a deep breath to gather his thoughts and said, "You tossed and turned last night, were you uncomfortable?"

She stared up into his eyes, "How would you know how I slept?" she asked. "As a watchman, I look for more than predators and thieves, but also to the safety of the people in my care. You're my responsibility until I deliver you to your father's house," he retorted.

She looked down and said, "I do believe this is yours." as she handed him his mantle. She admired it because it was well made, and a deep blue color with little stars of David weaved in here and there. It was very warm, lightweight, and it had a faint smell of a spice. She had noticed that all his clothes were well made. His satchel and sandals were thick cowhides with well-stitched uppers. The satchel was a rich caramel color from some of the finest leather, but made for durability. She held up the cloth that was lying next to her when she woke up.

It was a beautiful sea blue color, neatly folded lying next to her head.

"Is this yours also?" she asked.

He responded, "No, it's yours! I accidently set fire to your veil last night and… I… had this extra cloth…" He couldn't find the words to explain. She was staring at him again; it unnerved him.

She said, "Is this for your wife, I would hate to take it?"

He quickly corrected her, "No, it's not. It's payment for the other veil," He calmed himself and said, "During the cool of the night, I noticed that you were shivering so I covered you up." He recalled, with subtle joy, that when he did, she rolled over and wrapped herself in his garment without waking. He smiled to himself. "How is your forehead?" he asked, noticing she had a bump and bruise. She said it was fine, and thanked him for his care and concern for she was quite unaccustomed to it.

"Well, you will be glad this stumbling, bumbling woman will be out of your care this afternoon!" She said as she prepared the food.

"Quite the contrary," Manni said, "You have been a fresh breeze and cool water[14] to us all. Your singing, laughter, conversation and excellent cooking has made this trip wonderful, and I won't forget it or... you." Lamarra stiffened. She noted the husky tone in his voice and, when she looked up at him, how his deep brown eyes held her gaze. He continued to express his gratitude and appreciation for all she did for him and his crew. He thanked God she was there. He had answered their prayers! She had never been appreciated like this before. She thanked him and called the men over to eat. They all gathered around, waiting eagerly to see what she had prepared. Manni blessed the food and Lamarra served Manni first and then Obadiah. Obadiah was surprised because he normally ate last. She told him that they would honor him today for his past works of doing all the cooking on the road. All the men said Amen and laughed and ate their fill. She would miss this band of shepherds and the comradery they had for one another. Everyone was ready to go after they ate and Manni led them out. He looked around for

---

[14] Lamarra- (French, Latin) means from near a pool

Lamarra, and she and Obadiah were talking about how to cook quail. He was trying to get her to give him her secret recipes. She wasn't giving in too easily. Manni caught her eye as he looked back for her to join him up front, but Obadiah was questioning her about seasoning quail. She nodded if she should come up with him and he shook his head for her to stay with him. They were all starving for feminine attention. She smiled back at him warmly and continued to harass Obadiah. She pondered all the good things Manni had done for her. Now, she hoped to find good things awaiting her in Sychar.

CHAPTER FOUR

Time passed quickly as they walked to Sychar. Great weather and good company made the journey pleasant. They took turns escorting Lamarra and asking her for cooking tips. It was a joyful time that was quickly coming to an end. The gates of Sychar had caught Lamarra's attention. The sun was high in the sky and hot on their heads. They looked forward to resting in the shade and having a cool drink. The men said their goodbyes, and then went to the well to water the flock and rest in the shade. Manni helped Lamarra remove her bundle off the donkey and walked with her to her parent's house.

He saw she was concerned and asked, "Is something wrong, Lamarra? You have a worried look on your face."

She said, "I'm sorry. It's just strange that mama would be cooking inside on a hot day like today." They looked at the smoke coming from the chimney. She continued, "Well, I can't thank you enough for all you have done for me. I hope we see each other again." Manni was struggling with his emotions right then. He was tongue tied and afraid.

He managed to say, "You're welcome. The pleasure has been all mine. We must replenish our supplies from the market, and after we rest, we will be on our way to Caesarea Maritime. I will stop by and honor your parents before I leave."

She said, "Oh, why don't you come now. They would want to meet you."

He said, "I will give you some time with them first, because the smoke has made you curious. I'll stop by before I leave." She went to the door tentatively and knocked.

"Mama? Its Lamarra." Manni tried to hide his concern for her. She was worried, and he wanted to know what was going on in her parent's house. He tried not to pry, but he saw the concern on her face. He watched her as she walked to the door and knocked. The door swung open and her mother greeted her with a hug and a kiss. She looked thin and haggard. Lamarra hugged and kissed her back, but she was shocked by her mother's appearance. They went inside. Manni knew right then that they weren't going anywhere until he found out what was wrong with her parents. He went his way into the marketplace to give them privacy and to see what wares they had.

The heat was stifling in the house. She looked around for Abba and saw him in the next room. She asked mother how she was because she was so thin. She brushed aside the comment and asked her what happened to her forehead.

Lamarra said, "A little injury" and demanded to see Abba. She called to him, "Abba, are you awake?" He stirred from his sleep, and couldn't believe his ears.

"Lamarra, is that you, my child?" She went in the next room where the fire was roaring, and he was wrapped in every blanket they had. Mother had even thrown a rug over him. His leg was propped up and covered. She was sweating already from the heat. She knelt down and kissed his face, he was cold; she was scared.

"Abba, how are you? What's wrong with your leg?" He pulled an arm from under the covers and cupped her face.

He said, "Glory to God for answering my prayer. What happened to your beautiful face, my daughter?"

"Oh, nothing Abba. What happened to you?" She pulled back the covers on his leg and saw it was swollen and oozing. It was starting to smell.

He said, "I was visiting a family in the country and tripped and tumbled down the hill into a thorn bush. I got scratched up pretty bad. My leg was pierced by a thorn, which will be hard to get out for a few days."

Lamarra turned and looked at her mother and asked, "How long has he been like this?"

"Two Sabbaths ago, and it's gotten worse over the last two days." Lamarra's mind was racing, thinking of all the spices and plants she would need to help Abba. She searched the house for anything to use.

She said, "Mama, you have very little food here and no provisions, what has happened?"

"We were running low on things when your father injured himself. He has been so sick I haven't dared to leave him for a spell." She saw the fear on her mother's face. She hugged her mother.

"Don't worry mama. I'm here now." She grabbed her veil and she said, "I'm going to the market to get a few things you all need. I'll be right back." She kissed Abba on the forehead and rushed out. As she went, she ran into neighbors who were glad to see her and inquired about her father's health. She said he was doing fine but still weak, but she had to get some things for him at the market. She made her apologies and rushed on. She was on a shopping frenzy: lamb and organ meats, garlic, onions, kale, lentils, and a variety of spices. She mumbled to herself "I need something for his pain[15] so he can sleep." She was running out of money and left the rest at the house. She haggled the seller down to the lowest amount, but she still didn't have enough money.

A familiar voice came from behind and said, "Sold! We will take it!" It was Manni, and he gave the seller the money. Lamarra was so grateful. This man was always there when she needed help.

She said, "Thank you so much. I will repay you when I get home."

He saw the worry on her face, "How are your parents?" She told him that Abba was injured and mother hadn't left the house since. It was a mess. Mom was exhausted, and Abba was no better. She was afraid for them.

He walked back with her to the house and said, "What can I do for you, Lamarra?"

She said, "I don't have time to get fire wood and water[16]. I need to cook and to get the house in order. If you could get the water and fire wood, if you don't mind, I would be forever grateful."

---

[15] Matthew 27:34
[16] Getting water is normally women's work.

He said, "Consider it done." She gave him a water bag from the house. He took her hand and encouraged her.

"It will be alright, Lamarra. The Lord always sends help[17]." She believed him and watched him walk away. She went in the house and started to cook dinner for her parents. When she got back home, she took a closer look at his leg. She gave him something for pain, cleaned it up, and then let him rest. As she cooked, she told her parents how she got here with Manni. They knew it was the hand of God that brought their daughter home at such a time as this! Her father just laid there listening to his daughter talk, and her mother kept praising the Lord with every miraculous detail.

Manni knew in his gut they were staying in Sychar tonight. He couldn't leave Lamarra and her parents in this condition. He went to the well and told one of the men that they would stay the night and leave at first light. He would be helping Lamarra with her parents if they needed him. He got the water and the wood and returned quickly. There was a knock at the door. Lamarra ran to

---

[17] Psalms 46:1

open it. Manni walked into a sweatbox. The smell of onions, garlic, sweaty bodies, and sickness all rolled up in one slapped him in the face.

Lamarra introduced him, "Manni, this is my Father, Scribe Hosei, and my mother, Miriam."

Manni dropped everything and bowed to her father and said, "Honor and peace to this house Scribe Hosei. May God's blessing and prosperity be to you and your family!"

The old scribe said, "Come forward I want to thank and see the man who cared for my daughter all the way from Joppa." The Scribe sat up on one arm as Manni knelt.

He looked him squarely in the eye and said, "I'm told you honored my daughter while on this trip, and were a blessing to her, is that true?"

Manni nervously said, "Yes," and began to defend himself. "I've known of her for years in the marketplace of Joppa. She was highly respected, and she was always gracious. While we were on the road I was personally responsible for her welfare. I know she has a cut on her forehead... but... she tripped on something before I could get to her. But no one has harmed or molested her in anyway, sir. I give you my word."

Scribe Hosei said, "Thank you for protecting her, and I do hold you to your word. I'm sorry for the condition you found me in but, I hope we will speak again before you leave."

"Yes sir, I will make sure of it." Lamarra prepared a plate for her father and her mother. Lamarra and Manni stepped outside into the cool evening air. She left the door open to allow a breeze to flow through the house.

"Lamarra, what's the matter?" He saw she was about to cry, and his heart went out to her.

She looked away from him and said, "I didn't want to come home because I was afraid of what my father might think of me, and I find them like this! Oh my God... what if I didn't come? What if I went elsewhere?" He grabbed her shoulders.

"Lamarra, it's a good thing you did come. They need you like never before. I truly believe God is directing our steps, although we have no idea where He will lead us[18]."

---

[18] Psalm 37:23-24

"You're right." she said, "Could I trouble you before you leave to help me with my dad?"

Manni looked in her eyes and said, "What can I do for you, Lamarra?"

"I want to get my dad freshened up and make him comfortable."

He said, "I will wait out here until you call me." She rushed inside and gave her mother some warm water to wash her father with. She checked his wounds. After draining some of it she mixed some herbs together with the myrrh for a poultice and bandaged his leg. She called for Manni and he came in and followed whatever directions he was given. He picked up the old Scribe and placed him on the mattress in the next room while his daughter scrambled to freshen up his bed. Hosei thanked him for his help.

Manni asked him, "How'd you hurt your leg?

He answered, "I was coming back from visiting with family and tripped and fell down the hill." Just then, Lamarra walked up and Manni looked at her and they both smiled and shook their heads. Manni said, "I can see that happening," and winked at Lamarra.

She smiled and said "Ok, let's get you settled for tonight." Manni lifted the scribe with ease and placed him on his fresh bed. Lamarra gave him a cup of broth with the myrrh in it, and encouraged him to rest.

Then she turned to her mother and said, "Your turn!"

She laughed and said; "I think I can handle this myself now that Hosei is resting." She shooed them out of the house while she attended to herself. They walked outside into the cool of the evening.

She took a coin from her girdle and said, "Here is the money I owe you."

He humbly refused, and said, "All the cooking you did for us! There is no chance I will take any money from you. What you didn't know is I work for food."

"What are you talking about, Manni?" as she giggled

"If a man doesn't work he doesn't eat[19]; So, I work to eat. With you doing the cooking, I'll do whatever you want just to eat what you've

---

[19] 2 Thessalonians 3:10

prepared." She laughed, but she had tears in her eyes.

He asked "What's wrong, Lamarra? Why are you so sad?" Tears rolled down her cheeks.

"I am so grateful to you for all you have done. You have helped me at every turn, and I am so thankful to you for all your help." She touched his arm gently.

"You are the most honorable and generous man I have ever met, and I appreciate you. May God bless you richly and abundantly for being a blessing to us." She looked at him so lovingly.

He took a step toward her and she backed away and pulled her hand behind her back. "HE'S MARRIED!" she screamed in her mind!

"Well, thank you. Remember, I work for food, so if you need anything, I'm your man!"

She smiled and said, "I remember, you're the one that can eat a horse!"

"That's right," He said. "Now go and get some rest. I'll stop by in the morning to check on you all. Good night!"

Lamarra went into the house and everyone was sleeping peacefully. The stale oppressive air was gone and Lamarra was alive with hope. She slid the widow's coin out of her girdle and placed it back in her purse. She sat down and promptly fell asleep.

CHAPTER FIVE

Lamarra arose early, and during her prayer time, she inquired about why Manni was in her dreams.

This time, Manni was arguing with a man, and she tried to stop him. When he pushed her aside, he had been punched in the face by the other man, and this caused her to wake up abruptly.

She asked the Lord, "why was Manni, a married man, in my dreams?" He is married, and his wife is one blessed woman to have a man like that! She had to remind herself that he belonged to another woman, because it was easy to get lost in those deep brown eyes.

She began cooking a meal. Her father was still sleep but her mother awakened and helped her to prepare the meal. She kissed her on her forehead, next to the scar, and smoothed her hair back.

She said, "God answered my prayers and he sent help, but I never thought it would be you! I was afraid we would not see you. I was hoping someone was going to Joppa so I could get word to you, but I never made it to the marketplace. Praise the Lord, here you are! He knows what we need, even before we ask." She asked her mom to heat some water and she would wash Abba's clothes on the roof after breakfast. She gathered the linen and took it to the roof. The air was crisp and a little breezy. She looked around the city and noticed much had not changed. People seemed less friendly and a few of the older people had died. Their children occupied their homes or moved on. She wondered what her fate would be. When her mother called then she came back in to the house. Abba was awake.

"There's my lovely daughter!"

"Good morning, Abba," Lamarra said, "How do you feel? How's your leg?"

He said, "I feel stronger this morning. Thank you for helping your mother and me. God sent you right on time! Matter of fact, I think I'm hungry!"

"What would you like to eat, Abba!" He said, "Stubble tastes good when it's made by your hands, Lamarra!" Everyone laughed. She made fresh bread and seared the lamb just the way Abba liked it. There was a knock at the door and she opened it!

"Manni!" she said, "What is all of this?" The women helped him to unload his arms.

"Blessings and honor on this house Scribe Hosei. I honor your home due to you daughter's hospitality to me and the crew on the road. We wish to bless this household as she blessed us! These provisions are for you!" They quickly unpacked the provisions: a leg of lamb (salted and wrapped to preserve it) onions, garlic, fresh fruit, vegetables, a small container of myrrh and another one of honey. "The men contributed when they heard you were sick Scribe. Please, accept our gifts and bless it. If there's anything else you need, we will get it for you before we leave."

Abba said, "Manni, you are truly kind and generous please stay and have a meal with us."

He said, "No, I don't want to intrude."

Hosei said, "You are not intruding. We insist that you stay. Your kindness deserves honor and I know you love Lamarra's cooking."

"Indeed, sir I do." They sat, ate, and he told stories of this trip and others prior.

Abba asked him about his family, he said, "All I have is a daughter named Ilani[20]." Just then, there was a knock at the door. Her mother opened the door and it was one of Manni's men; the one who was always following Lamarra around.

"Blessings and honor to this house. Sorry to disturb everyone, but I came to be a blessing to Lamarra for her good cooking on the road." Lamarra glanced at Manni and saw his irritation with his worker. Lamarra jumped up and invited him in. He nodded to everyone and honored her father.

---

[20] Ilani- means sunshine

55

He glanced at Manni and said, "I didn't get an opportunity to contribute when the men where together, so I thought I would bring it before we left." Lamarra thanked him for his thoughtfulness in bringing bread and dates. Manni was very irritated with this little puppy sniffing around Lamarra. She thanked him for his kindness. Manni stood to his feet and thanked Scribe Hosei for his hospitality and, of course, the ladies for the great cooking. They said their goodbyes and he told the men to break camp and leave out, and he will catch up with them. Everyone walked outside as Ariel was walking toward them waving her arms.

"There you are Lamarra! I heard you were back." She said

"How did you hear all the way out in the country?" Lamarra responded.

"Those rivers and streams carry more than just water. A little fishy told me."

Lamarra responded, "The little fishy wouldn't happen to be your handmaid at the well yesterday?"

As they talked, Scribe Hosei called Manni back into the house.

"Manni, I have a question to ask of you."

"Certainly scribe, what is it?" Manni replied.

"Are you married?" he asked.

"No sir, I'm a widower. My wife died in child birth 5 years ago." Manni added.

The Scribe apologized for bringing it up. "So, you have a daughter? How old is she?"

"She's almost 8-years-old."

The scribe told him, "When I met Miriam I was just like you. I couldn't stand for another man to even look at her. I wanted to kill him. God helped me with my jealousy, and he will help you with yours. I can see you love Lamarra. Now, what are you going to do about it?" Manni was stunned by her father's directness.

He stuttered, "She is mourning, and I thought it too soon. I'm just a shepherd and farmer... I'm not worthy of her."

Hosei told him, "Manni, I don't know how much time I have left, but I'm going to bless you and give you permission to marry her. I know my daughter, she cares for you and you're just the man for her. I know you will make her happy and take care of her, as you have already demonstrated to us. There is very little of her dowry left, but you are well able to take care of her. I thank you again. son; whatever your decision is." Manni was surprised he called him son! "You will always be a son to me, for you cared for me and my family. The Lord and I will never forget your kindness. Can you get that box for me? Hand me that bottle on the shelf. I want to anoint and pray for you before you go." The old Scribe nearly drowned him in oil and prayed for him like a father would. Manni hugged the old Scribe and blessed and honored him and his house. The Scribe said to him, "I know you are Jewish Manni."

"How did you know?" Manni said surprised!

"You have the star of David sewn into your mantle. Don't worry; it's just what God desires, that we would be one nation worshiping him[21]. Go in peace my son." He hugged the old Scribe again, not wanting to part with the fatherly embrace he had longed for. He walked outside wiping oil off his forehead.

Lamarra said, "Aha, he got you. When the anointing falls on Abba, he lets it pour on anyone

---

[21] Exodus 3:12

close by!" Everyone laughed. "You will be greasy for a month." Miriam hugged Manni and thanked him for his help.

Ariel saw she was a third wheel and quickly excused herself to look in on Scribe Hosei by walking by the house saying, "Be warm and be filled[22]!" Manni and Lamarra walked toward the well. His mind was racing.

"Should I say something now." Lamarra interrupted his thoughts and said, "I hate to see you leave…" That sweet tender voice pierced his heart. "I've come to depend on you, and who will rescue me from my clumsy feet? Mama says Abba and I walk like pigeons," she laughed. "Your wife and child will be overjoyed to have you back."

"I have no wife!" he said. Angrily, Lamarra said, "You told me you were married, and you have a daughter."

"No, I didn't say I was married and yes I have a daughter" he stated calmly.

"You asked me to pick out something for your wife!" she shouted back.

---

[22] James 2:16

59

"My wife died, and yes I asked you to pick something out for... the next wife...whoever... she will be. I wanted to see what you would choose." he moved closer to her looking in her eyes.

"All this time I thought you were taken... married... and ..."

"And what, Lamarra," he said in that husky voice as he stood close to her gazing into her feisty eyes "...and what?"

"And I thought you belonged to another... and... and... I thought I could never have you," she said softly.

He said to her, "I thought you were consumed with grief for your husband and didn't notice me!" You've been married to rich merchants. What could I possible offer you?"

"True love," she said as she leaned towards him and he kissed her slowly and deeply. She fell into his arms and melted in his embrace. His arms where strong, yet tender, and she fit perfectly[23]. She gripped his body not wanting to let him go. He parted from her and searched her eyes.

---

[23] Genesis 2:22

"Lamarra, you are more than any man deserves, will you be my wife? I'm not rich like you're …"

She cut him off, "YES, I want to be your wife for the rest of my life[24]." He kissed her releasing all his passion on her. His mind exploded. She forgot where she was; he loved her and wanted her. He couldn't leave her now. He snatched himself away from her and she staggered on her feet. He pulled her arm and said, "Come with me!"

She said, "What's wrong? Where are we going?"

"Back to your father's house." He knocked on the door and they entered in. He said, "Scribe Hosei, bless this house and I honor you and your household. I ask permission to marry your daughter and to be her covering[25]. I have the bride's price[26] with me, but I can bring the gifts once I return home. I ask that you accept this until I return in one month to celebrate and receive my bride."

---

[24] Elephantine contracts; husband and wife for ever
[25] Ruth 3:9
[26] Genesis 34:12

Scribe Hosei looked at his daughter and asked, "Does this please you, my dear? Will you take this man as your husband?"

Lamarra was crying and said "Yessss, Abba. I will have him as my husband." Miriam was praising God and jumping up and down.

"Let's have a covenant drink[27]." The Scribe gave Manni and Lamarra a cup of wine and had them drink from it. He didn't want to go, but he had to get back.

He told them, "I have to return home to finish the business for my trip. I will return in one month for my bride and we will celebrate! Scribe Hosei, get well so you can travel to your daughter's marriage celebration in Caesarea." He pulled Lamarra close to him, looked in her eyes and told her, "I never thought I would find someone to love again, then God gave me you. I can't wait for you to meet Ilani, my daughter. She will be 8-years-old this fall. Excuse me Scribe." He kissed her again. "By the next moon we will be husband and wife! I must go catch up with my men! I love you, Lamarra," he said as he darted out the door.

---

[27] John 6:56

She ran behind him, "I love you Manni." She watched him as he hurried to catch up. He turned around to get one last look at her. He had to tear himself away from her or he would not leave. He was excited and had to get home to start the preparations[28]. He caught up to the men and spurred them to hurry to Caesarea Maritime. They all wondered what had happened to him!

---

[28] Ruth 4:11
John 14:3

CHAPTER SIX

He arrived late the next night. The house was asleep, except for his steward, who was always alert upon his return[29]. He knocked gently, and the door opened.

"Welcome home, master," his steward said. Manni always felt self-conscious being called master.

"You are your own master, Johanan[30]. Surely, I don't need to remind you," as he pulled at his ear[31]

---

[29] Luke 12:36
[30] Johanan means: Jehovah is gracious
[31] Deuteronomy 15:16

helping him with his mantle and his shoes. Manni grimaced, "How are you my friend?"

Johanan responded, "I am well, sir. Your trip was prosperous I gather."

"Yes. In more ways than I could have ever imagined." He handed him a lamp and he shuffled to his room, weary from his trip. Everyone was asleep, and the quietness was relaxing; when suddenly he was attacked from behind by a little person squealing with laughter.

"You didn't see me or hear me," she laughed. He grabbed her up in his arms and swung her around and kissed her face repeatedly. Ilani promptly gave him a scowl and pointed to a place on her cheek that he missed, and he quickly kissed it repeatedly. She squealed with delight and hugged him tight. He returned the affection. She said, "Okay Abba, I forgive you for staying away so long."

He looked in her beautiful eyes and said, "Thank you, oh gracious princess for sparing my life. What can I do to make it up to you?"

She said seriously, "Never leave again!" The directive was not lost on him.

"Well then, I guess I shouldn't give you this gift, so you won't expect anymore," he said with a chuckle. She started frisking him, trying to find his pockets on his girdle and looked in his sleeves. She was tickling him trying to find it. He laughed with ease, falling across the bed. She kept probing him until she saw him look over at his satchel. She popped up and flipped over him and off the bed like a desert rabbit running for its life. He rushed to his satchel, and they both played tug of war with it. She rummaged through it and pulled out a doll wrapped in the same material it was wearing. It was a pretty light blue material with orange-knotted dots on it. The doll had long black hair made of goat's hair with a beautiful tunic and veil covering her face. On her little wrist and ankle were bracelets made of colored thread and seeds. She was a beautiful doll.

Ilani gushed, "Ohhhh Abba, she is beautiful. I love her." He laid across the bed watching every little expression on her face. He loved these moments with her. She was so happy and funny! Her happiness was the most important thing to him.

She wrapped her arms around his neck and nuzzled his ear and said, "Thank you Abba. I love you!". He grabbed her up and started kissing her all over again. She squealed with glee. She started frisking him again.

He said, "What are you looking for little girl. You got your present, leave me alone and let me be."

"Oh no you don't, Abba. I know there is more here somewhere."

She pulled everything out of his satchel, and he told her "It's not there." She went over to the bundles and rummaged through them, and found a pretty little pouch with small bracelets. It had orange and red beads and a blue and orange shawl with tassels on it. She put on the bracelets and wrapped the shawl around her.

"Abba, I love everything you brought me back. It's beautiful." As she modeled her wares, he sat back and laughed at her pretend grown up movements. She pulled the cloth across her face like a veil, under those almond shaped, thick long lashed eyes. He was hooked with just that one look! She was captivating to be so young. She would be a beauty in a few years, and he spoke out loud before he realized it.

"What am I going to do with you, Ilani?"

She giggled and said, "What you always do, take care of me."

He said to her, "That's a guarantee, but you have made a mess of my room with your selfish treasure hunt and tossed my belongings everywhere! Can I get freshened up before you assault me again?"

She giggled, "That's okay Abba, I'll help you clean up. That's the least I can do for you" She looked over her shoulder at him and got him again with those eyes. He chased her out of the room with her arms full of beautiful wares. He closed the door and pick up his satchel and a knock was at the door.

"Come in." It was Johanan. He knew just what Manni needed. He had a large pot of hot water, which he poured in the large vessel in the corner. He hurried and returned with a plate of cheese, bread, fresh fruit, and a glass of wine. He sat it on his side table and asked if there anything else master needed. Manni said "No, thank you Johanan. Good night."

"Good night sir." He slowly disrobed, stepping behind the dressing wall in case of a sneak attack by his daughter. His thoughts went to Lamarra and how much more joy she would bring to their lives. He stepped in the large floor basin and dipped the bowl in the large bucket of warm water, and poured it over his head. It was so refreshing. He loved to travel, but he hated the dust. It got everywhere and in everything. The men thought he was upset leaving Sychar because he was pushing everyone so hard to get back. The truth was he could not wait to see his wife again. He told no one of his plans. He needed time to clear his mind and think about what needed to be done, because every thought he had was of kissing her and looking in those brown eyes. He was crazy to leave her behind, but maybe that was best, because it would be hard to not to know his wife[32]. He dried his hair and applied some of his anointing oil. The hint of cinnamon infused his hair. Cassia[33] had made the

---

[32] Genesis 4:1
[33] Cassia- a type of Cinnamon

oil especially for him! Her purpose for making him the oil was so she would be with him wherever he went. "The aroma will remind you of me and I will always be on your mind." she would tell him. During times of great loneliness, the delectable scent would bring precious memories of Cassia.

Manni continued to keep the tradition alive for Ilani to know her mother in a small way. Now the old Scribe baptizing him in a fresh anointing that was enough to last for a year.

He thought, "Maybe I don't need any," and laughed. He pulled on the fresh linen tunic, lounging coat, and sandals Johanan had prepared. He reclined while he ate and thought of his brief time with Lamarra, how they met and immediately connected with one another. The old Scribe peeped his shortcomings, but encouraged him to let God help him. Like he said: he knows what it looks like in him. He was amazed to see her at the market after he just saw another operated her shop. He always admired her. She was good to her customers and always laughed and joked with them. Many husbands went to her for suggestions on what to purchase for their wives. They must have been good ones because they kept coming back. She had chosen something for him and his wife had loved it. He wondered if she had any children and if not, what happened? What happened to her husband? He was much older than her and a seasoned traveler. Now that he was alone he could think about what he wanted to know about her because when he was near her, he couldn't think straight. There was a little knock at the door. He answered the little intruder, "Come in." Ilani ran in the room jumped in the bed and snuggled under his arm. He bent over and kissed her head.

She said, "Abba, I missed you a lot. When you didn't come home by the Sabbath, I was afraid, and Sarah told me to pray to Yahweh to protect you and bring you home safely. And He did!! He heard me!"

"Yes, he did baby. He has heard all of our prayers and answered them too!" The child chattered on about her days without him and how she helped Johanan and Sarah around the house.

She said, "Ester came by to visit Sarah, and was trying to get her to talk about who you wanted to marry, and did you like her."

Manni snapped back to reality, "Hold on little girl. What are doing spying on adults talking? You give Johanan and Sarah their privacy and stay out of their business. Do you hear me noisy?"

"Yes, Abba. I was good, Abba. I obeyed them while you were gone. I didn't climb any trees and I didn't beat up Samuel when he trespassed on our fields! It's our land and he should not be on it!"

"Ilani, stop it. It's the Lord's land and we are stewards taking care of it, just like Johanan and Sarah take care of us. We are all like them to God. We are responsible to take care of what he gives us[34]. And stop fighting with Samuel, he's a nice boy."

"Yes, Abba, but we must do better, so he will be pleased!" Manni looked at her. Where does she get this?

"He is already pleased because you obey and worship him. Now obey me and go to sleep!" She hugged him and kissed him good night and sniffed

[34] Genesis 2:15

his hair for the familiar fragrance of his anointed oil. She snuggled deep into his chest and promptly went to sleep. He thought, "How am I going to get Ilani out of my bed and Lamarra in? I wonder what she is thinking right now."

CHAPTER SEVEN

"8-YEARS-OLD! AN 8-YEAR-OLD! What am I going to do with an eight-year-old? They are bossy and stubborn."

Hosei stopped her, "Death and life are in the power of the tongue,[35] and you won't like the fruit of it!"

"I'm sorry, Abba. Forgive me, but you know what I'm talking about."

He looked her in the eye and cocked his head and said, "I dare say I do," and laughed. "You reap

---

[35] Proverbs 18:21

what you sow my dear," he laughed so much that his leg started hurting. Lamarra was still ranting.

"He didn't say he had a child."

Both her parents responded, "Yes, he did."

"I mean," she said, "he didn't say she was 8."

Hosei corrected her, "And she'll be 8 in the fall."

She glared at him. "I thought she would be twenty and married with her own children."

Her mother piped up, "He doesn't look that old, Lamarra. Just calm down. It will be fine."

"Mama, that's what you said about all my husbands, and this is number 5. Abba, I'm telling you now, I am done. If this doesn't work out, I don't care what the law says I will never marry another."

"Careful daughter. Make no vow with your tongue that you cannot keep[36]."

"Abba, I'm serious. I love Manni like none other. He has treated me better in a few days than most of my husbands did all of their lives! How could I marry another? Abba, I have been having dreams, and Manni has been in them. I think we are destined to be together. I first saw him in the

---

[36] Numbers 30:1-16

markets of Joppa where he would purchase fabrics and beads for his wife. He was well known to the men in the market and always brought his sheep, goats, and other things to sell and trade. A seamstress in town would meet him occasionally, and he would buy dresses and wraps from her[37]. He was very friendly, honorable, and always willing to help. The merchants spoke highly of him that he was fair but a shrewd sell. His men were never far away, and they too were respectful. A few years ago, he was seen in the marketplace here and there. They said he looked haggard and sick. He was one to stand off to the side and watch the people and their activities sometimes. It was as if he was searching for someone. He had been seen getting off the ships in Joppa sailing the Mediterranean to faraway places. He had traded livestock and fabrics and leather goods too! He had not been seen for a few years until now. Not as tired and travel weary but something was troubling him. The weight of the world was on his shoulders. One thing I know about Manni, he had always had an eye for nice things. The clothes he wore were well crafted and

---

[37] Acts 9:36- Dorcas

made to last. His mantle, an excellent cloak, light weight but very warm." Her parents looked at each other and then at her! She said nervously "...uh I was cold one night and he threw his mantle over me and when I awoke the next morning, I had never slept so well." They just looked at her and didn't say a word. She went on, "If you look closely, you can see the Star of David weaved into the mantle here, wonderful, so divinely detailed. His satchel is made of some of the finest leather. I remember there was a tanner in Joppa who did excellent work. He always wanted people to come over to see his product, but even the breeze from the sea could not blow away the horrible smell of his tanning agents[38]. Most people waited for him in the marketplace. There is a well-dressed man under those traveling clothes. I always wondered about him. Who was he looking for? Then he would suddenly leave...with a scowl on that brooding face."

Hosei said to her, "So it doesn't bother you that he is a Jew?"

---

[38] Simon the tanner Acts 9:43

"How do you know he's a Jew, Abba? He could have purchased the cloak for its quality and not the design!" Lamarra defended him. "Because I too saw the stars and I asked him!" Her mother gasped.

"Hosei, how could you permit this marriage to a man who would scorn and treat our daughter like a dog?"

"Miriam, are your eyes failing you. This man did not kiss OUR daughter in MY presence like someone who hated her."

Lamarra defended her husband, "He loves me… he not only told me several times, but he HAS SHOWN me, shielded, protected, lead, guided, comforted, scolded, provided for, cared for me, all in a few days. That's got to be love! He gave freely of himself and his treasure at all times and expected nothing in return… except some food… he works to eat. Anyway, Abba, yes, I will have him any day because he has shown me what love is. We both love God. We will have to decide where we will live as well as where we will worship."

"I agree, Lamarra. I spoke with Manni privately and I am confident that God's hand is truly in this union[39]. This man loves you and could barely leave your side. Trust the Lord, Lamarra. Manni is a good man."

She agreed, "When I finally decided to risk coming home, I went to the well and the market early that day. I had been praying and asking for God's help and guidance. When I got to the well, there he was, leaning against the wall, watching people. He inquired about the booth and I told him my husband died and the oldest son inherited the booth and sold everything." Manni knew what that meant. The children inherit everything, and they did not have to do anything for the stepmother. If the husband made no provisions, she had nothing. She was forced out after the time of mourning with her meager possessions. He noticed the old clothes she had on. He didn't understand. When she worked the booth, she was always well dressed and gorgeous. He would do anything to make a denarius.

Manni said "My sympathies to you. Do you plan on getting a new booth? You were very good at selling your wares and you have an eye for

---

[39] Matthew 19:6

quality." Lamarra thought to herself, *apparently not in men.*

"No," she said, "I don't have the connections my husband did."

Manni was curious now, "So what are going to do?"

She said, "I'm doing what the law says: I should return to my father's house[40]. I haven't been home in years, but the Lord will help me." She asked him, "Where are you headed?"

He said, "I'm headed to Caesarea Maritime." He was furious. That dog, how could he treat her like this? She is wearing rags. After all the money she made for him, this was all she had to show. He felt sorry for her. She saw the pity in his eyes, but he had no idea that she was glad to be free. A slave had better treatment. Ezra was a mean, greedy pig. She was glad to be leaving the gilded cage. Trapped in a loveless, childless and hopeless marriage. The only joy she had was talking to the customers daily. It was fun and exciting to hear of their exploits and travels to far places, but Ezra was always suspicious. He didn't like any man talking to her

---

[40] Leviticus 22:13

too long without buying anything. He called her lazy, demanded she have his food ready when he wanted, and if she didn't sell anything, she'd pay for it in other ways. As long as he made money, he was happy. If he didn't make money, he was mean and evil towards her. He would force himself on her when she didn't make a sale, and if it wasn't her woman's time she had no excuse, because it was her duty to him. So she continued to make him rich. She would wear the merchandise to entice the customers and he would sell it right off her back. She was stunning when she dressed up, and she did that all the time to sell whatever she could. He would showcase her cooking when he met with traders and he would expect a great discount because her food was so good. She had food, shelter, and a few clothes[41]. When she thought she was pregnant, it scared her. What would he do when he found out? He seemed to like the idea that she was barren. No mouths to feed, no little ones in the way, and no inheritance to leave behind. He could keep all the money for himself. He gave her only what she needed because he could care less.

---

[41] Deuteronomy 10:18

She hated her life. Would she ever find someone to love her that would want a barren, used woman? She feared her fate! When she had become pregnant, she was so excited. Four husbands later, and she was with child! She couldn't stand to smell flowers, and the nausea in the morning was the worst. She tried to hide it from Ezra, but He noticed she looked sick and told her to go to the other room and sleep there. He didn't want what she had. She was grateful for the separation. She could sleep in peace without the assault on her for wifely duties. He cared nothing for her or condition, just satisfying himself. He constantly reminded her of his husband rights and her wifely duties. He used sex to dominate, control, and humiliate her. When he realized she was pregnant, he became even more abusive. He hated the fact that she was pregnant. He made her life a living hell. He was trying to make her lose the baby. He accused her of trying to trap him and ruining his plans. She would pay for not being barren. He would scold her for not getting or doing something and make her scurry to get it and then trip her on purpose. He finally succeeded in his wicked diabolical plan. He caused her to fall. This time she couldn't brace herself in time. Her contractions started. She called for him to help her, but she knew in her heart he wouldn't come. He walked out of the house when he heard her cries of agony. She gave birth to a stillborn baby. She wept for hours. Then she cleaned her child and wrapped it up as if he were alive. Then she cleaned herself up and waited for Ezra. When he came home the next day he didn't even check on her. He sat in the front of the house.

She walked out to him and handed him his son and said, "You killed him. Now you name him and bury him." She was sick of it. She wanted to kill him. The other women in the marketplace figured him out long ago. At first, they were jealous until they saw how he mistreated her. They saw his tricks and sneaky maneuvers to embarrass her, so he could abuse her. She would scurry in the house and not be seen for the rest of the day. She would appear and wear a veil or be limping around. It was all to break her spirit. Everyone she met, loved her. The kindness she showed drew people to her. She was genuine in her concern, and they felt her love.

He hated that and tried to break her spirit. He felt
he owned her and humiliated her constantly. There
was no relief from her tormentor. His abusive
barrage continued even after the baby. She would
learn to worship him if it killed her! But God; she
prayed to be free from him. Several times she
seriously thought about killing him herself, but she
remembered the law: vengeance is mine said the
Lord and I shall repay[42]. Ezra was on a buying trip
in Assyria and was killed. His friends said he had
offended another man's wife,[43] and he killed him
for dishonoring her. How ironic. Consequences
are swift in Assyria. After the men told her the
story, they thought she said nothing because she
was in shock about his death. She could not believe
she was free! Tears streamed down her face. The
Lord had finally come to rescue her from that
horrible man, who would prey on his own child for
his selfish gain. Nothing was precious to him
except his god Mammon[44], which he sacrificed his
child and wife as a love offering. The loss of their

---

[42] Deuteronomy 32:35
[43] Deuteronomy 5:2
[44] Matthew 6:24

child and his brutality toward her was over. The last four years seemed like death itself. She wailed a heart wrenching cry for the child she never knew; the one person she longed to meet. What would his eyes look like? What would've been the color of his hair? Would he have her disposition or his father's business sense? She would never know. She wailed, for her child, for herself, to wash out all the pain She cried to release the hurt and shame; she cried to unburden the unbearable; she cried to be heard by God! The wailing women[45] joined the chorus of the grief of loss of life, her child, her husband and her years. They wailed with her, mourned for her and with her. The sound was heart piercing. It cut you to the core to hear women wailing for their loved ones. It was a haunting sound. Some knew her pain; they had sat where she sat. They knew because they lived through it, and they survived! For days she slept then awakened, cried, wandered about, and prayed. For weeks, her life was a dream, a fog of existence, purposelessness. Her tormentor was gone but a new one prevailed: guilt! She got what she wanted, but there was no satisfaction, no

---

[45] Jeremiah 9:20- grieving women

relief, and no comfort. She was expecting the worst, which was to come. His sons, Joiakim and Salu arrived. They were cut from the same cloth. They fell upon the shop like marauders, more than mourning sons. They accused her of killing him. Ezra was an excellent bookkeeper, he watched over every mite. They took everything: money, clothing, cups, merchandise... all of it! They only left her with a few of her personal items. They sold her booth to another merchant. She had a fortnight to get out! But the LORD in all his goodness sent a widow to her booth. She watched her step sons remove all and anything of value and spoke to Lamarra harshly. When she was able to casually walk by and spoke to Lamarra. She reminded her that if she ever needed shelter that she was always welcome in her home. She would not be a burden but a comfort to her and she was welcome. Lamarra accepted her offer and said she would be their tonight. But she would be going back to Samaria soon.

"Lord, you are my help to get back to my father's house. Protect me and guide me." She purchased some food and filled her water skin. She was ready to start a new life. She hoped her parents were well. She knew they would be glad to see her. Abba would feel bad for her because she had no husband and children again. What punishment had she brought on herself? It had been a year since Ezra's death. Hosei wept for his daughter as he overheard her conversation with her mother. God stepped in and answered her prayers. Now, her present emotional and financial condition needs healing. However, she seemed to trust Manni. Most women would hate to see a man coming after treatment like that! Lamarra seemed her old self, no outward scars, anger, or bitterness. He listened as Miriam encouraged her daughter in the love of God, reminding her that he had come to her aid in so many ways. She asked her, "Isn't it like the Lord to place Manni in the city on the day she was leaving. The Lord ordered your steps to your new husband. He's a good man, Lamarra. He truly cares for you. Just think, when's the last time your father went to the well to get water for us?" They both laughed.

Hosei chimed in, "I heard that!" Lamarra reflected, "Mother, he is so helpful, attentive, and he appreciates me. He really cares, but does he just want a mother for his daughter? The way he kissed you, I don't think he's only looking for a mother. The way he looks at you, Lamarra, there is desire in his eyes!!!"

"You mean lust, right? I've had enough of that and I'm not taking that anymore."

"Calm down Lamarra," her mother smoothed her ruffled feathers.

"He loves you and desires you as a wife."

"I hope so." she said, "He never mentioned his child before. But I do feel safe and comfortable around him. I'm at ease when he is near. There is so much to do before the wedding. Abba, you need to get well so you can enjoy the celebration!"

CHAPTER EIGHT

Manni was up at sunrise for his prayer time. He looked around the room to prepare a list of things for Johanan and Sarah to get started on. Ilani was sprawled over the bed. She had slept under him all-night. He had to see Malachi and Seth that morning to complete their business and return home to make the wedding preparations. He freshened up and got dressed behind a screen, realizing it would not do for Lamarra. He needed something more feminine and appealing to the eye! He was rearranging the room to accommodate her needs. She didn't have many possessions now, but that would change! When he went into the great room, Johanan and Sarah had a meal prepared. How did they do that? They were always up before him, seeing to his needs; it was amazing. The aroma of their favorite Arabic coffee was wafting through the house. He and Johanan enjoyed their coffee together. Sarah didn't like it, she joked about it putting hair on your chest. Manni asked them to sit down because he needed to talk to them. He told them that he was getting married next month and needed their help to prepare the house and Ilani for her arrival. He told them a few things about Lamarra, and that there was a lot of work to do especially with Ilani. They were excited for him because they knew the years had been long and lonely. The lights went off in his life the day Cassia died.

He didn't want to leave her alone on that horrible day. Her family would be arriving soon to help with her delivery. She still had a few months before that time. Cassia persuaded Manni to deliver a few goods to the next town and to send someone with a message to her family.

He didn't want to go but she assured him she would be fine for the day, and to stop worrying and acting like an old mother hen. So he headed out at first daylight.

She packed some food and kissed him and he was on his way. But he kept looking back and she would wave to him to reassure him.

Cassia was feeding Ilani and starting to prepare everything to get ready for Manni's return to a wonderful supper. She noticed she had a little water remaining in the pot. She grabbed the water pot and Ilani and headed for the stream. The bank was a little slippery, so she walked over to a rocky area where the current was stronger to catch her water. Suddenly, Ilani who was behind her, stumble and rolled down the bank in to the stream.

Cassia jumped in the stream with an awkward landing and rushed after her. She finally grabbed the little one's foot and pulled her into her arms. She was breathing fine, actually she was laughing as if she enjoyed the exercise. She kissed her face repeatedly and said, "I love you my joy, my love, my sunshine."

Ilani giggled and kissed her mother back.

Cassia went to walk up the bank to the grass and slipped in the mud. She fell hard on the ground with Ilani in her arms. She was slow to get up and felt a sharp pain in the pelvis. She just sat there for a minute and got her bearings. She needed to get back to the house and rest, so she poured out half the water to make her load lighter and had Ilani walk for a short distance. She started to have contractions, so she hurried home.

She calmed herself and prayed that Manni would return early with her sisters as she reclined on the bed and tried to relax with Ilani. She felt her contractions lessening so she rolled over to get more comfortable, and felt the baby moving around as well. She rubbed her stomach to comfort her child and shortly after her water broke.

She rolled on her other side to take the pressure off her lower back. Then when a sharp pain occurred in her belly, she couldn't move any more, and tried to stifle her scream not to frighten Ilani who was playing by her side.

Then another contraction hit stronger and before this time she knew that the child would be born today. She prayed for Manni to return! She worked through each contraction as it washed over her. Ilani had come closer to comfort her mother as she moaned during each contraction. Cassia tried to keep them both calm and quiet. She couldn't stay in any position long. It had been hours since Manni left and more before he returned. She just had to relax and stay calm and work through each contraction. Ilani kissed her face to comfort her mama she too knew something was wrong...she was afraid. Cassia started to sing a song that Ilani liked and she started to hop and dance around. Would she dance at her wedding would she dance again with Manni? Don't panic now... stay calm she told herself. She repositioned her weight and warm fluid gushed from between her legs she looked down and dark blood and clots where on the bed. Something was terribly wrong... OMG help me... Something is wrong. Stay calm she kept saying stay calm. She worked thru the next contraction and tried not to push. She kept saying Manni come back.... Lord send him back. Manni had arrived at the first house to make his delivery and the family was happy to see him. They loved hearing the news and the stories. But they saw he was preoccupied and worried about his wife. They encourage him to go home and they would get a message to her family and deliver his other goods for him. Manni raced back home as fast as the mule would go. He prayed all the way home that all would be well, but he couldn't get rid of the feeling in the pit of his stomach that something was terribly wrong. He prodded the mule to go faster all the way home. He rode up to the house calling Cassia's name with no response.

"Ilaniii" he called out and then he heard crying, he burst through the door and yelled, "no Lord!!!"

Cassia was pale and lifeless on the floor in a pool of blood. There was a trail of blood from the bed to the middle of the floor. She still had her arm through Ilani clothes so the child could not escape her. He kissed Ilani quickly and attended to Cassia calling her name to get any response from her, he screamed at her and shook her... and she aroused to consciousness.

"Cassia talk to me," he said. "what happened, what should I do."

She said, "I slipped and fell getting water and Ilani out of the stream. She said, and my birth pangs started. I tried to be still, but my water broke. The baby is stuck… I have no strength to push."

Manni was shaking, there was so much blood he was begging her, "What should I do… Cassia tell me what to do?[46]

Cassia said, "my strength is gone. I can't push anymore. Manni I love you, take care of Ilani and yourself."

Manni said, "no don't say that… tell me what to do?" He went to check for the baby. He recoiled at the sight, blood everywhere the baby was covered in it, he attempted to grab the child, but it was slippery with blood. He wiped him off and saw his buttocks and genitals. It was a boy. He saw the cord tucked under his arm. His legs, head and arm were still in the birth canal. His hope was defeated. He grabbed his son and attempted to reposition him, and more blood flowed out, it was dark red followed by red blood. Manni panicked, "no… no, no, no… no Lord, help her lord, oh my God help us lord… Cassia… Cassia… Stay with me… CASSIA…

---

[46] Women and known midwives assisted in childbirth not men.

He had turned into another man that was angry, depressed, and he started to drink, but Ilani rescued him. She demanded his attention at 3 years old. She went everywhere with him as if she were losing her dad too. They were best buddies. Ilani was used to having him to herself. She even started to walk like him, with long stride but with short legs. It was hilarious. Whenever she thought hard, she would furrow her eyebrows and mumbled to herself, just like Manni. She had all his mannerisms down packed by the time she was six years old. She knew the boundaries of their property by heart. She could use a sling and throw a rock to make the sheep fall in line. She gleaned after Abba and Johanan would cut the grain. She also liked spending time with Sarah picking berries and olives; she always enjoyed learning new things. However, hanging out with Abba was always exciting. He was teaching her how to ride a horse. Sarah didn't approve but she said nothing. Ilani was smarter and more accomplished than any boy her age. She needed to learn how to be a young lady. She counted money and bartered with the best of them. She was a bit much for eight years old.

Manni had to get her in line now, or no one will want to marry her! The thought of her being married troubled him. She was strong willed and bossy, which he felt was all his fault because he let her get away with it. Hopefully, Lamarra could smooth out the rough spot on her.

He gave the list of things to start doing to Johanan. He was about to leave when Ilani called him and asked him to wait for her. He went into his room, told her to stay in bed and get her rest. They had a lot to do when he got back. She hadn't slept the past two nights because she had been waiting up for him. She agreed to stay this time. She kissed his cheek and fell back in bed. As he rode over to Malachi's house, all he could think of was Lamarra, and if she would be pleased with him and how much she and Ilani would get along. She could teach her so much about being a woman. He admired her beauty and charm. She was funny, friendly, and everyone liked her. All he could think about was kissing her for the first time. His mind exploded with emotions and his body responded to her caress, it was hard to let her go!!!! She melted in his arms and she was a perfect fit. He was intoxicated at the thought of her. Her laughter warmed his heart. He could be happy again. He remembered every curve of her face. All the little movements and tilt of her head when she thought one was teasing her! He didn't even see Ester when he rode up, and she had called his name three or four times.

"I'm sorry, Ester. Good morning to you."

"Manni, how could you not see me with this beautiful dress on? Are you well?" Ester replied.

"That is a beautiful dress, Ester. I have business with your brother, is he about?"

"He's out back. Did you miss me, Manni? I missed you. I was desperate to see you. Did Sarah tell you I came to check on you?" She said as she ran behind him to keep up.

Manni said, "No, she didn't, but Ilani surely did!" He laughed, remembering her comments.

Ester was pouting now and said, "I do believe that little girl hates me. She is too mean to be so little! You really must teach her some manners, she is bordering on being rude to adults. She just needs a little discipline, and she will line up!" Manni made a note to himself to never leave Ilani in her presence alone.

"Excuse me Ester, while I speak with your brother." I'll wait for you to finish your business. Come and find me when you're done, Manni."

"Malachi, this house is getting so big, I can't find you."

"Grace and peace to you!"

"Good morning and God's blessings are upon you today." Malachi walked over and hugged his old friend.

"God bless you, my friend. I hope your trip was prosperous."

Manni responded, "In more ways than one. You are a rich man Malachi. I sold all your sheep and oils, with great expectations for next year. Jerusalem can't keep enough oil. They want twice the order again. "We will have to hire more men for there is much to prepare and little time to do it all."

Malachi, feeling the rush said, "Slow down my friend, one thing at a time." Manni put his share on the table, and sat in a huge chair Malachi purchased from Spain. He loved the carving and details on it.

He thought, "This would be a beautiful dressing screen in our room for Lamarra." He liked the sound of 'our room'. Malachi said, "Manni, are you listening to me? We must go to Tarsus and purchase the horses. Apollonius will give us a good breed and a decent price for a small herd, but we have to leave next month."

Manni totally surprised says, "I can't go next month."

"This deal is good now. He won't wait any longer for us. He's waited two months already."

Manni said, "I can't. You will have to go without me!"

Malachi stared at him, "Do you have sunstroke, Manni. He's your friend, and you made the deal with him and the timeframe. He's looking for you to come!"

Manni said decisively, "I have to go to Joppa, and I have business in Samaria."

Malachi said, "Why do you keep going there? They are a strange breed[47]. You can go when you get back." Manni shot Malachi a look that shut him up.

---

[47] Luke 17:18

Manni said "I have to be back in Samaria in one month to get my wife!"

Stunned, Malachi repeated, "Wife. You're getting married? Why didn't you say so? A Samaritan, really? Are you kidding? No, you wouldn't kid about that. Look at you, my friend. You are truly happy. Why the rush?"

Manni sat down and poured out his heart. "I can't wait. She is everything I ever wanted in a wife." He laughed, "The way she wrinkles her nose when she smells something. She can cook like no one I know. She can sing like a bird."

Malachi looked at him incredulously and said, "She's got you by the stomach. Manni you love to eat."

Manni replied, "I could drown in those brown eyes and be a happy man.

She is beautiful and smart." Malachi said, "She got you with the food. A Samaritan; how did you meet her? Do you know her father?"

Manni explained, "I met her years ago in the marketplace in Joppa. She and her husband sold some of the finest fabrics and wares. She would select some things for Cassia for me, and she loved them."

Malachi sighed, "she's a widow. Ester is not going to like this. She's had her eyes on you for years."

Manni said gently, "She's a sister to me, Malachi. We all grew up together. I'm sorry, I could never love her."

"Ilani will love having a mother. How are we going to get you back for the wedding?"

Manni, scheming in his head, "We can take some extra men and sail to Tarsus, purchase the horses and they can travel down the coast. I will catch a ship back home and go get my bride. I pray everything will work out. We can celebrate here. He told me my prayers are heard."

"Who said that?" Malachi asked.

"I saw him again, in Jerusalem." Manni said. "They say he's a prophet! His words touched my heart. I felt the joy to live again. He told me to forgive my father, because he didn't know what he was doing."

Malachi asked, "Did he know your father?" [48]

---

[48] Matthew 6:14

Manni said, "That's just it. He is too young to have known my father. Malachi, He is a prophet then. Uele was a hard man. I was afraid of him. He was mean," Manni said, "He was a good man, before he divorced my mother. Some rabbi told him he had to divorce his foreign wife to have eternal life[49]. He was angry with everyone, including God. He loved her. She had been the perfect wife, but he knew she didn't love him. However, she honored him and always showed him respect. She could cook, sew and take care of him. He didn't want to lose her. He married my mother when I was four years old. She was working the field and he was traveling along going to look for work. He saw her struggling with the mule and stopped to help. She fixed him a meal as payment and he never left. He was angry he had worked the land, built a life with this woman, was a father to her child, and now had to leave. He didn't understand it, or God. When he realized I would inherit everything he worked hard for and got nothing, he could not fathom it. He refused to

---

[49] Deuteronomy 7:3-4
Ezra 10:10

103

leave, and he took it out on me and beat me whenever he had an excuse. He called it discipline to make me into a man. My mother would console me and sing. She told me I would be a great man: a chosen vessel for the Lord. Blessings were due to my obedience and mercy. She told me about my true father Immanuel who was a Jew, who loved me and desired me to be a man of integrity and honor. That my vats and vineyards would be full.[50] We loved the Lord, Yahweh, and worshiped him only. My new stepfather's heart was broken. He had suffered great loss and abuse. He had tried to redeem himself, but he needed God to redeem him, not man. 'Love and respect him my son' my mother would say." [51] Manni spent a lot of time at Malachi's house to avoid his stepfather. Malachi's father was a trader and took the boys everywhere with him. He would bring things home to bless his parents, and his stepfather would get jealous of his son's opportunities. He was away on a trip when his father took ill. He asked for him constantly. When Manni got home his father begged his

---

[50] Deuteronomy 6:11
[51] Deuteronomy 5:16

forgiveness and told him how much he loved him as his own son.

"I love your mother, although she doesn't love me. I know these things. She gave her heart to your father years ago. I speak blessings over your life. You will be a great man of God. You will be what I couldn't be: a respected, wealthy man with a good family."

They buried him, and his mother mourned him for a short time and focused all her attention on Manni. She showed Manni where the land deeds were and the divorce papers that they never signed. His father's seal that he used to purchase some land, and Manni's name was on it. She had safely hidden the money of his inheritance. It was his! Uele came with nothing and left with very little. He worked hard to be a prosperous man, and she loved him for it. His mother's heart belonged to Immanuel, Manni's father. He was the very image of his father, tall, dark, and handsome. He was solid build with broad shoulders and his mother's eyes. He loved God and his mother.

Malachi commented that Manni was right: there was no time to waste. The festivities were approaching quickly. "I'll ask which men would like to accompany you to Tarsus and return with the horses."

Manni said, "I have to see Seth, and I'll see who he can spare to go with us." He completed his business with Seth, and headed home thinking of Lamarra the entire way there. Ilani met him in the stable.

"Abba, what is Johanan building? And why is Sarah busy cleaning and getting rid of old stuff? What is going on? Are we going somewhere?"

Manni tried to change the subject. "I'm hungry, aren't you?"

"I just ate Abba. What's going on?"

"Ilani, come and sit down so I can talk to you." She followed him in his room, climbed into his bed, and waited for him to speak. He sat next to her and her eyes were fixed on him awaiting his words.

He said, "Ilani, I love you more than anything, and always will. Things are changing constantly, and we'll need more help as the farm and business gets larger. All of us need more space. Also, I need a wife and you need a mother."

"I don't need a mother," she said with a direct stare and a matter of fact tone, "and you don't need a wife. I'm here for you and take care of you, Abba. I always pray for you and help you."

Manni was slow to speak, "Yes you do sweetie, but I need a wife for me. To look out for my needs… to talk to about adult things."

Ilani said very bluntly, "Sarah takes care of you. Why do you need someone else? Aren't we enough for you, Abba?" Manni tried to explain himself to this sweet seven-year-old.

"Yes, you all are enough for me as a daughter and as a steward, but Sarah is Johanan's wife, not mine." She jumped off the bed and pondered his dilemma.

"You're just missing mama, that's all! I know, I miss her too!!! Abba, it's hard for me to see her face anymore." Tears were streaming down her face. "I can't see her face, Abba!!!! I want to see her again." Manni began to panic. This was going bad – quick.

"Lord help me to help her. What do I say?" All he could think was to scoop her up and hug and kiss her. "You can see her again, by looking at

107

yourself. Remember that shiny brass mirror I gave you?"

"Yes, Abba."

"When you look in it you will see mama, because you look exactly like her! You don't forget what you look like so you can't forget her! I love you baby, and nothing or no one can change that! I love Lamarra, and asked her to be my wife. We are making room for her in our house and in our hearts. You will love her. She is beautiful, smart, a great cook, and a fun lady. She will love you because you are my wonderful, beautiful little girl. I will be leaving to go to Tarsus to get some horses. I'll return home and then go get my bride and we will celebrate when we return."

She broke away from him and said angrily, "No, Abba. Don't go!! I don't want a mother, and you don't need a wife. I'll be good, I promise. I'll clean my room and help Sarah more. I'll stop beating up Samuel and be a good girl. I promise, Abba." She was crying hysterically. Manni's heart broke. This was not a punishment. It was a blessing to have a mother and wife!

He grabbed her and spoke sternly, "Ilani, calm down and stop crying and listen to me!" She calmed down, sat on his lap and wiped her face. "Ilani, honey I love you and Lamarra. She will love both of us and be a part of our family. We will be a complete family again. Daddy needs a wife to come home to as well as a beautiful daughter, and when I am not around, you will always have Lamarra here, loving you. I need your help Ilani. I can't do this without your help. Will you help me?"

She grabbed his neck and said, "Yes Abba, I'll help you. I love you, Abba."

"I will always love you. When you are old and have children Lamarra and I will love you, as we do now! Now, let's get this place together, and the first thing is your room!"

"My room, Abba? What's wrong with my room?"

"First, you are getting too big for it. Your dolls need their own space. And you will be a young lady soon, with all of your jewelry and things, you know!"

"Abba, we do that stuff outside."

"Lamarra and I need more room for her and her things."

Ilani looked around and said, "You need a bigger bed Abba, so we can all fit in there. Lamarra needs a place to sleep."

Manni looked at her and said, "This is not going to be easy."

Ilani said, "No, it's not. You've got stuff everywhere, Abba!" Manni shook his head and left the short boss to tidy up the place. Sarah called Ilani to help her in the kitchen.

She responded, "I'm picking up my things now."

Manni said, "You heard Sarah, go help her with dinner. You can do this afterwards." Manni went out back and found Johanan with the mules gathering timber and boulders. When he saw Manni walking up, he stopped working and bowed to him. Manni dismissed the gesture and jumped in to help.

He said, "Master, I am so happy for you. I'm sure she is a beautiful woman to get your attention. As well as a good cook, as Sarah says, you love to eat."

"Because I work hard for my food! Because I work to eat." They laughed.

"I'll help you as much as I can to get the foundation up before I leave for Tarsus in Cicilia."

"You just got home, sire." Manni said, "I forgot about the horses from Apollonius. The mare should have foaled by now, but it will be a great wedding present for both of my girls. I don't have much time to spare because my traveling days will be over for a while[52]. I sail to Cicilia to purchase the horses and send the men home with the herd along the coast. I will return home by ship and prepare to go get my bride."

He had a sheepish grin on his face and Johanan said, "Yea master, go get your bride!"

---

[52] Deuteronomy 24:5

CHAPTER NINE

He arose early, and Ilani was right under him all night. What was he going to do? He prayed for hours for his wife, child, household possessions, and the trip and business. Johanan was already up with a meal prepared and waited for his master- his friend. He wasn't close to anyone else, not even his wife. He truly loved Manni, respected, and honored him. To be his servant was to be a king's counsel. They worked well together, and he always gave him a share of everything he did. He insisted on blessing him. When he enlarged the rooms, he enlarged theirs as well. Sarah loved it, but she still desired her own home. They would not be alive today if it wasn't for Manni. He saved their lives on more than one occasion.

The cup of Arabic coffee was hot and strong. Manni's father in law served it to him long ago and he loved it. As they drank their coffee he gave Johanan last minute instructions on the house. He would try and conclude his business quickly and take the next ship back to Caesarea. The men would bring the horses back to Malachi until he returned. He wanted to surprise them with their horses. Johanan rode with him to the port. He knew to expect him back in seven to ten days, so he could leave and go get Lamarra. It was a tight schedule, but he said he would be back in one month for his bride. He always tries to keep his word.[53] He and the men were the only passengers on board the ship. The water was a little choppy, but they had good wind in their sails. They would make it to Tarsus in good time. Four of the men had never sailed before and were seasick most of the time. Manni was used to sailing, going to new lands and experiencing new cultures. He loved it!

---

[53] Numbers 30:2

Because he knew the seas could be uncompromising and make passage difficult. He prayed for mild weather and a safe passage. They caught a swift current and arrived in Tarsus in two days.

Apollonius was a horse breeder from Greece. He sent his servants to meet Manni at the port and escorted them quickly to his home. It was a beautiful home on a hill and surrounded by rolling hills. The servants brought them into the courtyard and they scurried about seeing to their every comfort. Water was brought in for them to freshen up. Wine, bread, cheese, and fruit were brought in to settle their stomachs and satisfy their hunger. Manni went over to Caleb and asked him how his stomach was because it was his first time on a ship. He was glad they were riding back on land. He enjoyed the pampering, relaxation, and their hospitality, but Manni was impatient and paced the floor. Finally, Apollonius came out and greeted his guest. He walked up to Manni and hugged and kissed him[54]. Then his wife, Adonia, walked out like she was floating on air. Every man in the room was astounded at her beauty. She walked directly

---

[54] Genesis 29:13

over to Manni and kissed him on the mouth, much to his embarrassment. When they did that it made him uneasy, and they loved it because they knew he respected them and would do nothing to hurt them. She hugged him and wouldn't let him go. He blushed because he was so humbled.

They welcomed their guests and told them to make themselves comfortable, and assured them that the servants would see to their every need. They wanted to speak with Manni privately. They were good friends and genuinely cared for one another. They admired each other's gifts and talents that they used with such diligence. As they entered the private quarters, the children swarmed around excited to see the only man they considered an uncle. They assaulted him by jumping on his back, hanging around his neck, and asking thousands of questions at once.

"Where's Ilani and when is she coming?" They asked. They inquired about what gifts he had for them. They pulled him away from the children and sent them on an errand while they spoke with Manni. They could tell he was impatient.

"Sit for a moment." His private chambers were furnished with tapestries and decorative panels. No Spartan arrangements here. For he loved all thing of beauty. "My friend, sit and tell me what troubles you. You haven't stopped pacing since you got here. What is wrong!"

Manni spoke hurriedly, "I'm sorry, Adonia. I'm on a tight schedule and I can't stay. I have to hurry back to Caesarea..Because I'm… getting married."

They shouted for joy. Apollonius said, "Who is this goddess who has captured your heart! She must be beautiful and an excellent cook!"

Adonia said, "I'm so happy for you Manni." She kissed him again on the lips, and he blushed. She must be an amazing woman to grab you up. Manni unloaded his feelings to his friends and all his expectations and happiness for his union with Lamarra.

Apollonius said, "Let's celebrate now and drink to your happiness and eat and be merry." Manni declined the offer for now. He said his men did not know and he would tell them when they got back at home.

"I'm preparing things at home and I told her I would be back in a month."

"You don't have much time to get the horses back; it's almost a two-week ride back to Caesarea."

Manni said, "I need to catch a boat tomorrow and head back home."

Apollonius said, "I will send one of my men to find out if a ship is leaving tomorrow and make any necessary arrangements for you. Now, let's take care of business so you can relax a little and enjoy." They walked through the gardens to the stables. There was a staff of men there to care for the horses. Humans wish they were cared for so well. As Manni and Apollonius talked, one horse neighed and kicked the stall. They all turned towards the ruckus.

Apollonius said, "We better let him out before he breaks down the stall." One of the helpers went to open the stall. Out scampered a beautiful white stallion with a black main, tail and sox's. He trotted right over to Manni and nuzzled him and almost knocked him down. "Champion." Manni grabbed the horse around the neck and hugged and kissed him. They were so glad to see each other. The horse pawed the ground, ready to fly with his friend.

"How are you my friend, I hear you are a father several times over since I've seen you last!" The horse seemed to understand what he was saying! It was amazing.

He kept nudging him, Manni kept saying, "No, I can't. I don't have time." Finally, the horse bowed before him, so he could mount him.

Apollonius said, "You might as well take him for a ride because he won't let you rest until you do!" Manni climb on his bare back, and Champion took off at galloping speed as if he was stealing away his friend; like this time together will not be shared or interrupted. They watched as a rare partnership was celebrated between animal and man. They never saw a horse so glad to see a person before. They rode like the wind, animal and man stretching forward to the next mile in perfect stride and balance with each other. The plains were beautiful against the mountainous range before them in all their majesty. They finally stopped, and Manni got off and walked with his friend. He told him all about Lamarra and how much he loved her and had to get back home to marry her, so he could have more children.

"I hope we can, because she has no children of her own." When they returned to the stable, they were both soaked with sweat. Apollo was waiting for them. There were several beautiful horses with him, and Champion rode up to the mare and nuzzled her and nodded to Manni. Apollo laughed, "He tells you this is his lady Magnificent with her foal." Manni loved to see the family together. He was happy for his friend. Apollo said to him, "You know, I can't do anything with Champion. He just breeds for me and that's' it. Otherwise, he is moping around here for his friend. So, with that being said: I give him to you Manni, because he favors you anyway. You are his true master. My gift to you and the foal is a gift to my niece Ilani. Purchase the other 3 horses and Champion's mare. That's final. I will take no more than a bargain price. If it weren't for you, Champion would not be alive and we all know it. You nursed him back to health after the boar gored him. We thought we had to put him down, but you were persistent with him, and he is stronger than ever. Now, after siring six males and 14 mares, I think I got more of my share of his genes." Manni was overwhelmed at his friend's generosity.

He said, "Thank you, and God bless you for blessing me richly and abundantly. I will send word when we will celebrate our wedding, and you all must come down and meet Lamarra."

"Come in, freshen up, and we will talk." Manni went to his quarters that had that bathing room in it; he loved it! It was a shower with warm water coming down over him and a small pool if he wanted to bathe. He slipped into a fine tunic and went to check on his men. When they saw Manni, they were surprised because he didn't look like himself. They were all relaxing and satisfied with the hospitality. They remarked how gracious and rich his friend was. Everything here was beautiful, and his wife was a goddess! He told them to get their rest because everyone would be leaving tomorrow. He would be on a ship, and them on the road home with the horses. He went to his quarters and as usual, the children found their way to Manni. They played and laughed together until their father instructed them on the time for prayers and bed. Apollo sat with Manni and talked with him concerning his travel plans over the next few weeks. He warned him that the seas can be rough this time of year and very unpredictable. He advised him to go by land. Manni informed him that he had a date with destiny and he told his bride one month, and even that was too long in his eyes. He was desperate to see her again. Manni implored him to come to Caesarea in the spring for their wedding celebration. Everything would be ready then and he had to bring the children down. They would stay in his humble abode.

"Well, I can't wait to meet my new sister! I know she can cook because I know you my brother and she's got you by the stomach.

"You and Malachi won't give me any peace about that, but you are right."

"We work for food," They said in unison.

"Rest my friend, you sail early. A merchant ship leaves at dawn and will take you on. I will see that your men are properly furnished to travel home tomorrow. I will send escorts with them."

"Thank you, Apollo. I appreciate you and Adonia."

"Oh, I know my wife loves you. You are the brother she never had, and she knows she is safe around you. That's why she kisses you like that. You're the only one she can do that with. She is expressive with her love and people can misinterpret that. But you are honorable and respectful, and I think a little afraid of her." Apollo chuckled.

Manni said apologetically, "she always catches me off guard and her beauty is disturbing to me. I'm sorry, Apollo. You of all people should know what I mean."

"I do my friend. When I saw her, I thought she was a goddess from Olympus to test me. It was love at first sight. I couldn't breathe, and everything had stopped around me. I thanked the gods for allowing me this vision. She was with her family when I first saw her, and I was speechless for the entire day. All I could do was watch her every move. My father kept slapping me to snap out of it because it was impolite to stare, but they were used to it; all the women were beautiful in that family. You know the rest of the story, so yes, I understand. Adonia is overwhelming to the best of them and I understand you need to return to Lamarra. So, get some sleep and I'll see you in the morning." Manni slept thinking of Lamarra and Ilani as his new family. It was a peaceful night.

He arose excited and eager to sail off. He went to see his men with final instructions. Then he ate a meal with his friend and family. The children were not awake yet, so he, Apollonius, and Adonia had time alone. They discussed the wedding celebration plans for the spring, and last-minute details. Adonia kissed Manni goodbye and Apollo road with him to port. The morning was hazy and breezy; a storm was coming. Apollo asked him to delay his trip, but Manni hoped to beat out the storm. If the crew was confident, so was he. He was a man of destiny, and he was determined to meet it. God was willing and so was he! He pressed on saying his prayers. He boarded the ship and settled in for the voyage. The ship's crew had their work cut out for them to stay on course because the wind would try to have its way with them. At night, the storm raged and even Manni pitched in to help the crew maintain the sails. He helped as much as he could, but the waves were getting the best of them.

He continued to pray to the Lord that he would spare this ship and its crew so they all could see home. So he could start his life with Lamarra. Don't let her marry another!

"Lord allow us this chance to praise and honor you as a family, a mother for my child. Lord remember me!" The ship overturned. He swam to get away from the ship and the sails, but a rope had his foot and was pulling him downward. He released it, and came up for air, only to be pushed down by another wave. He saw a plank floating and swam towards it. As he reached out to grab the plank, the sea rose, and it hit him in the head. Everything went black!

CHAPTER TEN

She hurried to the other side of the city. She kept her eyes attentive for the physician. His wife said he was with a family at the end of town. Lamarra asked everyone if they had seen him. She was scared and didn't know what else to do. Abba was dying, and they had done everything. Maybe he had one more treatment for him. The physician stepped into the street as she turned around. She ran to him and begged him to come to her father's house because he had gotten worse. The leg was discolored and had a horrible smell. The fever was raging in him. When they talked to him, he babbled on and on and spoke the word of God. Their greatest fears had taken hold. Abba was dying.

As they entered the house, the physician could smell the culprit. Death had a distinct odor and it was residing here. He examined the old Scribe and pulled the family aside and prepared them for the worst as best he could. Even if he removed the leg, the disease had spread throughout his body. The fever would complete the job. They prayed more, repented more and begged more. It had been 30 days since Manni left, and she expected him any day now. This was not the celebration that she anticipated. This was a nightmare: the horrible smell, and a mother wasting away and clinging to her husband of 33years for dear life. Money was scarce, and it could not buy his life back. All they could do was help with the pain and wait with him. Abba had told her two weeks ago that he had a dream. He saw her wedding with Manni and they were so happy. She was a beautiful bride[55]. He said he would not be there because he was going before her and that was God's will. He assured her she would be fine because the Lord would make everything new[56]. He asked her to get the anointing oil, and he anointed her head until it ran down unto her feet. He laid hands on her and prophesied to the sons in her womb, those sons that she would bear that he would not hold in his arms, but he has held up in prayer. He prophesied health in mind, body, and spirit, and that her household would be blessed[57] and she would be a woman of plenty. Her husband would be an honorable and blessed man and he would care for his family until a very old age and he would prosper! She would reap where she had sowed. The blessings of Abraham were upon her. She was only able to stand by the power of God as he spoke to her spirit and encouraged her. She received every word into her spirit and recited it daily. God could do whatever he said because she believed he spoke through her father. This was her hope, that life would spring forth from her, and she clung to it.

God had prepared Abba, but mama was worried. She didn't eat and was losing precious weight. Lamarra couldn't even think about getting

---

[56] Revelation 21:5
[57] Proverbs 31

married, because everything had gone wrong. Death was at their door, but she craved Manni's strength and calming support. He would be a rock for her because she was ready to fall apart. The last few years, death was around all the men in her life, child, husband, and now father soon. She had to help her mother, but it was hard to stay strong. She went in the corner and cried. Abba heard her weeping. He called for her. "Lamarra, I need your help."

"Yes, Abba," she responded. "What can I do for you?"

He said, "You can be strong for me! I am so grateful to God for sending you here to help us. Take care of your mother because she is not well."

Miriam said, "Oh Hosei, don't worry about me. You get well, and I'll be just fine." The old Scribe took his daughter's hand and looked her in the eye and said, "I love you my dear and Manni loves you more. That man has bound himself to you already. He will never marry another because you have his heart. He will return! He is a man who keeps his word, and he will protect you always. I already gave him my blessing to marry you and cover you."

The next day Abba died. The weeping and wailing was unbearably heartbreaking. Her mother wept bitterly, until she passed out, and then woke up and started all over again. They buried him and cleaned the house. It was an empty house with the warmest soul now departed. She hated death. It was relentless and consumed everyone she loved. It was at her door too often as of late. Her mother could not get up out of bed. She was so weak and depressed. It had been six weeks and Manni had not shown up, and she was starting to worry. She was a little relieved that he wouldn't find Abba in the horrible state he was in, but she wondered if he had changed his mind, or found another. She even wondered if he had been attacked on the road or what?

Early the next morning a man knocked at their door. He was tall and burley with a pierced ear. He must be a slave sent by his master, she assumed.

The man asked, "Excuse me, I'm looking for Scribe Hosei and his daughter Lamarra?"

Lamarra answered, "I am Lamarra, my father died last week, can I help you?"

"Yes, ma'am. I am Johanan, Steward of the house of Manehillel. I am looking for my master." Lamarra's heart dropped, "Where is he?"

She cautiously said, "Manni left here six weeks ago with his men going to Caesarea." She had to sit down. Her knees were shaking, and she couldn't think.

Johanan said, "May I come in?"

"Yes, please." she said, remembering her manners. He was sorry he came; this was going to be bad news for all! He didn't know what to say or where to turn. Lamarra said, "This is my mother, Miriam, and my father Scribe Hosei died last week."

"Forgive me for intruding, and I'm sorry for your father."

"Where is Manni?" Lamarra insisted. "What is wrong… something is wrong…" Johanan felt horrible. How could he tell her?

"Lord help me to break the news to her gently." He said silently to himself. "I came here because he has not returned to Caesarea as he said he would. Ma'am, might I be so bold to say, you are a beautiful woman and I see why my master is in love with you. He was very anxious to get back to you, and I thought he might have changed his plans and came for you instead of coming home first. All of which is unlike him, to change his plans that drastically."

"Where is he?" she said hysterically.

He said, "He was coming back...?"

"Is he dead? Is he dead? What are you saying Johanan? Is he dead?" He tried to calm her fears, but he was afraid too! "Lamarra, I don't know. That's what I trying to find out. He had a business trip to make when he got back, and I've got men going to Tarsus to find out what happened when he left there!" Lamarra was getting hysterical.

"Tarsus... He was on a ship. Oh my God, no. Lord it can't be. Maybe he met another woman and stayed with her," she said. Johanan looked at her directly, and with the most soothing voice said, "Mistress, there is no way another woman could gain his heart because it belongs to you. His thoughts were always of you and his daughter. He has been striving to marry you every day since he left you. He was consumed with the wedding preparations."

She panicked, "Oh lord, help us. How is Ilani? She must be scared to death, the poor baby!"

"She is having a really tough time. He's never late in returning." She couldn't take another loss. Not after Abba. Her eyes filled with tears.

"Johanan, you know him better than I do, could he have changed his mind or went somewhere else at the last minute. Maybe he is hurt somewhere and can't get word to you." Her voice shook, she was shaking all over. She couldn't hold it together any longer. "Nooo, he's not gone. No my love is not dead. No Lord… not Manni…Oh God Help him!" She fainted!! Her mother and Johanan caught her before she hit the floor. Everyone was crying! Johanan picked her up and placed her on the bed. Miriam got a wet cloth and wiped her face. The shock was too much for her after all they had been through. He felt horrible about bearing bad news. When she awakened, she saw the little white stars of David on Johanan's dark brown mantle. It was just like Manni's.

She looked up at him and moaned, "Tell me the truth Johanan, what happened?"

"He went to Tarsus and he said he would turn around and sail back with the next merchant ship leaving. I went to the port and waited every day for him to arrive. One of the captains said there had been a shipwreck during a storm of a boat leaving Tarsus. I prayed it wasn't his. He never came home after leaving for Tarsus; he knows what that does to Ilani. He would not do that!"

"Maybe he's in Joppa," she said.

Johanan shook his head, "I went there already, and no one has seen him since he left with you. His men returned from Tarsus and said he sailed early that morning before they took the road back." She was shaking again. She couldn't hold it together. Johanan spoke softly, "I had hoped he was here with you because he was excited and anxious to be with you. I figured he couldn't wait any longer and came here first. I have people looking for him everywhere." She wailed even louder! "God, oh no not again. Not my love." She felt her heart ripping out of her chest. She said, "How is Ilani?"

"She was crushed. She hasn't stopped crying. She won't come out of his room. She stays in his bed all day. She hasn't eaten or slept in weeks.

That's why I came here." The big burly man was deflated and defeated by the loss of his friend and master. This was his last hope to find him alive.

He said, "Master's friend in Tarsus is sending ships out to look for him and he will send word when he finds some information."

She said, "That was three weeks ago." Johanan nodded his head, he was defeated. He had retraced Manni's steps and still could not find him. He refused to speak it, to say it, to admit it...that he was dead. How could it be! Johanan sat in disbelief of his friend and master being gone!

He said gently, "I must get back to Ilani. She will be waiting for me to return. I can't tell her this. I want to give you this." He heard in town that the family had fallen on hard times. He gave them some gold piece, something to help her during this time.

"I will stay in touch, but I have to get back," he said. "If I hear anything, I promise to let you know." She waited, but she dared to hope?

CHAPTER ELEVEN

Months had passed, and Lamarra had developed a routine of going to the market hoping to get work. She sold some of her food items, but they barely turned a profit.

She was on her way home and heard a voice say, "Hello Lamarra, how are you?" As she turned she saw a beautiful stallion and Caleb. He appeared lost standing there sheepishly She couldn't believe it.

"Caleb, how are you?" She was glad to see anyone connected to Manni. He awkwardly said,"

I have come to see about you, Lamarra. How are you? I heard about your father from Johanan."

She was genuinely glad to see him, "Thank you Caleb, for seeing about me. Is there any word about Manni?"

He hung his head, "No, still no word. I came to offer my help in any way I can."

"Well, we are running short on food. I will pay you back."

He said, "That's fine, Lamarra. Let's get what you need." and they walked to the marketplace.

"Your horse is beautiful. I've never seen a white horse with a black mane and tail, he is so big and powerful looking" The horse nodded in agreement, which surprised Lamarra.

She asked, "Does he understand what I'm saying, because he acts like he does?"

"He just likes you, that's all," Caleb said. He purchased the food for her and asked if there was anything else they needed[58]. She thanked him, and promised to repay him. She asked about Manni's daughter. Caleb said she was devastated and he saw very little of her, but assured her Johanan and

---

[58] Leviticus 25:35

Sarah were taking care of her. Lamarra fixed a meal and Caleb ate with them and enjoyed the hospitality. He complimented her on the meal. He said he would leave them to their evening and check on them in the morning. She thanked him again and he left. Miriam had already curled up in bed when Lamarra went to see if she needed anything. She said, "No. He likes you, Lamarra. He came back for you. Don't you see that? He was sweet on you when he was with Manni. Your bride's price paid the taxes and most of the loan Hosei took out on the house. Marry him, Lamarra. I won't be here long and he loves you."

"Mama, I don't love him. I could never love him. I'm done marrying to be married. I should be able to take care of myself."

"Are you serious? Are you living in the same town I am? These women would be glad to have someone to take care of them."

"But at what price?" she retorted? "There is a heavy price to pay for marrying the wrong man! I know what I'm talking about, and I won't fall prey to that again," said Lamarra.

"And every man is not Ezra," said Miriam. She told her to remove the brick in the wall where she would find a leather wrapper. Lamarra untied the strings and unrolled it. Inside was her parents' marriage contract, Bill of sale for the house, and her marriage contract to Manni." "Mama when... how...why... did Abba do this!" The contract stated that he had given 100 pieces of silver as a deposit for the bride's price and promised the other gifts upon marriage when he returned. Hosei and Manehillel signed it.

"Lamarra, any man who did what he did for you must be in love. That kind of care is generated out of love. The way he looked at you said it all. The bride's price Manni gave was enough to pay the taxes and most of the loan Hosei took out on the house. There is some left but not enough to live off for the rest of the year. The synagogue couldn't support all the priest and scribes, so your father wrote the legal papers for people for a small fee. Sweetie, you need a covering and I don't see anyone else knocking on your door," Miriam said closing her eyes to stop the conversation.

Lamarra said, "Good night, mama." She went outside in the cool evening and sat on a tree stump, and thought about what her life could have been with Manni. She could not accept his death. The likely hood of him being alive was slim, at best. She couldn't see herself married to Caleb. Manni didn't like him. He annoyed him for some reason. She didn't know why, but he was attentive and was helpful like Manni. Unfortunately, there was no one like Manni! In those short few days, he had shown her more love, kindness, appreciation, and faith than all her husbands combined. Every experience with him was passionate and new. She remembered awakening that morning wrapped in his mantle. She was warm and cozy with her face pressed against the hood, on which she detected the faint smell of cinnamon. She took a deep breath and inhaled the scent of his clothes. He covered her and he was protective yet thoughtful and considerate. The way he held her, gentle and possessive, but not demanding. That kiss was passionate and pleasing, not forceful and dominating. Those dark brown eyes staring into her very soul left every emotion and desire exposed to him. She could not hide her feelings when she looked into those intense orbs. She could deny him nothing when he looked at her like that; she wanted to love him, to experience the true love of a real man! And now, he's gone! Widowed four times, divorced once and still barren.

"I must be cursed," she concluded. "God, forgive me for whatever I have done for you to forsake me like this," she said as she wept bitterly!

Within the month, Miriam died. Lamarra couldn't take another blow by death. She had been beaten down by sickness, disease, and death. Loss was her only companion, and it was cold and empty. She was depressed and cared about nothing or no one. Weeks after burying her mother, she didn't talk much. She sat for days starring off into the horizon. People started to think she lost her mind!

Caleb had moved in on the rooftop, but always found a way into the house. He always had Lamarra's best interest at heart. He made her a proposition that as long as he was there on business, if he could pay her for food and lodging that would be the perfect answer to her problems.

She would have an income and a protector. People already shunned her because they thought she was cursed because anyone who came near her died. They began thinking she was prostituting herself because, now some man was living with her. No one could prove it, but it didn't look good for a scribe's daughter to have some man living on her roof and going in and out of her house every day. Caleb made remarks and advances toward her. He always complimented her and said what a good wife she would be and all she could do was laugh. If only he knew! What she didn't know is he had gone to the man who held the balance of the loan on the house. He told him that he planned to marry Lamarra and wanted the loan payment to be part of her dowry and bridal gift, but it would be a surprise for the wedding day. Seeing Caleb had been living at her house for months already he agreed and signed over the loan to him. Now, the trap was set.

He approached Lamarra one evening, while in the house to have shelter from the rain. She had fixed a delicious meal, and he was feeling like the big man. He told her how he loved her the moment he saw her and had desired her ever since. That he wanted her to be his wife and he would have her no matter the cost! Lamarra just stared at him and started to laugh hysterically, for a minute he thought her mad.

She told him, "You know that everyone has died around me, right? The town's people think I'm cursed, and I have buried more husbands than people have children, and you want to marry me? It's not healthy for YOU to marry me! I don't and will never love you Caleb. I appreciate everything you are doing for me but marriage is out of the question." She had put him off too many times. She had side stepped his advances and slipped out of his embraces on numerous occasions. He shouted at her, "Lamarra I love you. You have to marry me!" She looked him in the eye and said bluntly, "But I don't love you and could never love you because my heart belongs to a dead man. It's buried with Manni, wherever he is and that's where it will stay. I have nothing to offer you. I will suggest you leave because I have nothing to give you." Caleb was angry How dare she throw Manni in his face, he couldn't stand the ground he walked on.

Everybody loved him and thought he was the greatest person ever. He's dead now. He walked over to her and tried to stay calm and said, "Well you choose how you would like to live, as my wife or as my slave."

She said, "What did you say?"

"I own this house. Either you marry me, or you work for me, it's your choice. I will get what I have paid for and worked for, I deserve you! And I will have you one way or another. What say you, Lamarra?"

"There's no Manni to help me now," she thought. "Lord what did I do, and how did I get in this mess." She turned on him and said angrily, "For your sake, I will not marry you and I will not be your slave. You have no idea what death awaits you binding yourself to me. What kind of love is this that forces me in the street on in your bed? Quite the web you have weaved Caleb. Now I see why Manni didn't trust you, and I won't either. So, you want to lie with me, Caleb. I will lie with you as your concubine[59] not as your wife or as your slave.

---

[59] Genesis 21:14; 25:6, Judges 19:1
Concubine – a mistress staying in the house.

You shall lie with me when I say, and you will still sleep on the roof if you expect to get into my bed." He was shocked that she agreed to be his concubine, and he agreed quickly before she changed her mind. He tried to embrace her, but she said with hate in her voice, "Don't you ever touch me unless I say you can. You have no rights to my body unless I give it to you. If you expect to eat and lie with me, these are my conditions." He backed away and said, "It's still raining. Can I stay in here tonight?"

"Yes," she said, "you can sleep in the other room." He was glad just to be in the house. He scurried to the other bed, and told her good night. Lamarra could not believe what she had just done, but it was done. Now she knew why he was called Caleb. [60]

---

[60] Caleb- means bold, impetuous. Animal name meaning dog.

CHAPTER TWELVE

"Lord, things are not working out at all! I know I have sinned against you, but can you please make a way out of no way for me. I'm ready to try it, just you and me, on my own. I can't take it anymore." She looked up in the sky and at the harsh hot sun beaming down on her. Her veil was wrapped on top of her head as she walked toward the well. She didn't expect anyone to be around considering the heat. The last time she was here, she almost got into a fight with one of the women. "Thank you, Lord for sending Ariel to cool me down. I would have killed someone. I'm so tired of so many things

Lord. I'm tired of struggling, tired of evil looks, tired of wicked words by the women." Caleb's concubine was her new title bestowed on her by her loyal tormentors, and she was tired of him too. The merchants and sellers in the marketplace treated her like a leper. No one wanted anything from her, not even conversation. The world was being turned upside down.

"Lord when will there be peace, in my heart, in my life, and in my world. This sneaking around to avoid people is not the life I dreamed of. Is that all life is… a dream?" Shifting her thought, "No tears today Lord, I am tired of crying. It doesn't help. My heart is raw with hurt and pain. Only you can help me now, don't forsake me Lord. Oh, now who is this at the well! I'm not going to say a word to this person. His clothing is different, he isn't dressed like us!" As she approached the well cautiously, she realized this man was a Jew but not just any Jew. He dressed like a Rabbi; her father and the men of the synagogue would dress like that. She knew she would be considered a half breed or a foreigner[61].

---

[61] Luke 17:18 Mixed race, non-Jewish.

[62]Jesus spoke to her and said, "Give me a drink of water".

Lamarra retorted, "How can a Jewish man, like you, ask a Samaritan woman, like me, for a drink of water?"

Jesus replied to her, "If you only knew what God's gift is and who is asking you for a drink, you would have asked him for a drink. He would have given you living water."

The woman said to him, "Sir, you don't have anything to use to get water, and the well is deep. So, what are you going to get this living water with? You're not more important than our ancestor Jacob, are you? He gave us this well. He and his sons and his animals drank water from it."

Jesus answered her, "Everyone who drinks this water will become thirsty again, but those who drink the water that I will give them will never become thirsty again. In fact, the water I will give them will become in them a spring that gushes up to eternal life."

---

[62] John 4:7- 42

Lamarra told Jesus, "Sir, give me this water! Then I won't get thirsty or have to come here to get water."

Jesus told her, "Go to your husband, and bring him here."

Lamarra replied, "I don't have a husband."

Jesus told her, "You're right, when you say that you don't have a husband. You've had five husbands, and the man you have now isn't your husband. You've told the truth."

Lamarra said to Jesus, "I see that you're a prophet! Our ancestors worshiped on this mountain, but you Jews say that people must worship in Jerusalem."

Jesus told her, "Believe me. A time is coming when you Samaritans won't be worshiping the Father on this mountain or in Jerusalem. You don't know what you're worshiping. We (Jews) know what we're worshiping, because salvation comes from the Jews. Indeed, the time is coming, and it is now here, when the true worshipers will worship the Father in spirit and truth. The Father is looking for people like that to worship him. God is a spirit.

Those who worship him must worship in spirit and truth."

Lamarra said to him, "I know that the Messiah is coming. When he comes, he will tell us everything."

"Messiah is the one called Christ," Jesus told her, "I am he, and I am speaking to you now." At that time, his disciples returned. They were surprised that he was talking to a woman, but none of them asked him, "What do you want from her?" or "Why are you talking to her?" Then the woman left her water jar and went back into the city.

She told the people, "Come with me, and meet a man who told me everything I've ever done. Could he be the Messiah?" The people left the city and went to meet Jesus.

Meanwhile, the disciples were urging him, "Rabbi, have something to eat."

Jesus told them, "I have food to eat that you don't know about."

The disciples asked each other, "Did someone bring him something to eat?"

Jesus told them, "My food is to do what the one who sent me wants me to do, and finish the work he has given me. Don't you say, 'In four more months thee harvest will be here?' I'm telling you to look and see that the fields are ready to be harvested. The person who harvests the crop is already getting paid. He is gathering grain for eternal life, so the person who plants the grain and the person who harvests it are happy together. In this respect, the saying is true: 'one-person plants, and another person harvests.' I have sent you to harvest a crop you have not worked for. Other people have done the hard work, and you have followed them in their work." Many Samaritans in that city believed in Jesus because of the woman who said, "He told me everything I've ever done." So, when the Samaritans went to Jesus, they asked him to stay with them. He stayed in Samaria for two days. Many more Samaritans believed because of what Jesus said. They told the woman, "Our faith is no longer based on what you've said. We have heard him ourselves, and we know that he really is the savior of the world."

The town was a buzzing about the Messiah's visit. They were amazed that he came to them at all. Jews hated Samaritans, and the feelings were mutual. God had not forsaken them; he came down to see about them! He cared for them, loved them, and saved them. They were blessed. The gloom and doom had lifted over Lamarra. Over the past few weeks, people were kinder to one another, including her. They were embracing her and thanking her for bringing the Messiah to town. They forgave one another and truly loved each other. Life had sprung from hope! She could hope again. It was like a new day to her! Everything she had heard her father teach about God was suddenly clear. She didn't have to worry or be afraid. She could also forgive and let go! There was hope because God was on earth!

Caleb was in the marketplace getting provisions to leave for Galilee. He was going to try to benefit from the Rabbi's visit. The men were telling him that he was blessed to be associated with the woman who brought the Messiah to them. Surely, he felt compelled to change his situation. Of course, it was Lamarra who was the problem, not him. He was the patient suitor waiting on the love that was owed to him. She was glad he was going. He had been exiled to the roof for months now and he was frustrated with her. He figured some time apart would soften her heart. Obviously, he didn't understand her.

As she was talking with people and perusing the wares, she saw an Arab man leaning against the wall watching her. It was something oddly familiar about him. When she paid for her food and turned around to get a better look, he was gone. She quickly scanned the area and he was nowhere to be seen. Caleb was busy getting accolades about Lamarra discovering the Messiah. He loved the attention and prestige it brought to him in the marketplace. If she would concede to marry him, it would make everything right. He would be greatly respected by everyone in this town; even Lamarra would have to submit. The horse was suddenly irritated and prancing, Caleb placed the bundle on the horse and the food fell to the dirt. He yelled at the horse in frustration, then he tried to calm him, but he kept pulling away. Lamarra tried to sooth the beast, but he could not be comforted. He settled down a little, and Lamarra bent over to pick up the food. Caleb put his arm around her waist to show support, and slipped his hand to her buttocks to show his ownership of her. Lamarra recoiled from him and dodged his public display of affection.

"Now come come my dear let me help you, I'm only trying to serve you my love" he said as he groped for her.

He continued to stress his difficulties with both beast and wife.

Caleb said, "What do I have to do for you to submit to me?" He sneered at Lamarra for embarrassing him in front the men.

He grabbed her arm forcefully and Manni pulled her away from him saying, "Take your hands off my wife!"

Lamarra screamed "Manni! My love you're alive!" As she struggled to be free from Caleb.

Manni had not heard her say his name in months. She had his full attention.

He looked into her shocked, tearful eyes as they grew big and she yelled "Manni…" once more. Caleb punched him in the nose when he wasn't looking. The men held Caleb off Manni, which didn't take much effort. Manni was sprawled in the dirt trying to figure out what happened. The horse reared and flailed his forelegs to protect Manni.

Manni said, "calm down boy," and the horse calmed and leaned over to Manni to lick the blood running down from his nose. He thanked the horse.

Lamarra ran to his side, "My love, are you all right!" She was all over him hugging him and kissing him in the marketplace. Caleb was furious at the affront, and went to grab her again and the horse stepped in front of him and neighed and pranced. Everyone was amazed at his horse. Caleb backed off and commanded Lamarra to come to him. She ignored him, because she knew her prayers had been answered and her breakthrough was here. Lamarra was trying to help Manni up, but he was too heavy. The horse came over and extended his bridal to Manni and helped raise him up. He thanked the horse for his help and he snorted in return. Caleb seized the opportunity and pulled Lamarra to him. Everyone watched them, amazed. The Elders had been called because of the commotion and inquired to the problem between them. Manni was fuming. He knew he had to stay calm because he didn't want to lose her again. Caleb was relishing in his victory over

Manni. He might have to help him in that if he continued. After all, he would be defending his wife's honor, even if she was acting like a whore. He had a tight grip on Lamarra; he wasn't going to let this victory over Manni slip from his fingers.

Manni confronted him, "Caleb, you are a thief [63]and a scoundrel! You stole my horse and now my wife! You take your dirty hands off of her right now!"

The Elders stepped in and said, "that's a serious accusation you've made. We know this man to have lived in this town for months. Who are you to make this claim?"

"My name is Manehillel from Caesarea Maritime. Lamarra is my wife and this is my horse and I can prove it. Can you, Caleb?"

Caleb snarled back at him, "Yes, I can. Lamarra has agreed to be my concubine by her own admission, and I don't have to prove a thing to you."

The Elder interjected, "But you do have to prove it to us. We will meet tomorrow at the city gates and determine the truth of this matter.

[63] Exodus 22:1-14

Everyone come with your proof and your patience. We will tolerate no fighting. Now, go home." Caleb pulled at Lamarra and the horse.

Manni yelled, "Be careful how you treat my wife and my horse!" The horse snorted and stomped as if in agreement.

CHAPTER THIRTEEN

"Concubine! She agreed..." Manni kept hearing those words over and over. He could only stare at her. His heart was deeply wounded! What happened to make her agree to such a thing? Lamarra saw the hurt on his face. She wanted to explain, but Caleb was pulling her away from the man she loved more than life itself.

She kept pleading, "I can explain. Manni I love you let me explain."

Caleb was pulling the horse that wouldn't move until Manni said, "go with him for now." The horse snorted and made Caleb work to pull him down the street. Onlookers stared Manni up and down. A few people even recognized him.

Ariel came up to him and said, "Oh my God, Manni. You look every bit an Arab. I almost didn't recognize you. You look pretty good as a sheikh. Life's been good I gather." Manni had forgotten he still had on clothes he had gotten from the family on the island of Cyprus. He had to admit he was a dashing sight; all he needed was a saber. He looked at Ariel, hurt and dejected, with confusion written all over his face. She felt sorry for him because he wasn't going to like the news. She didn't want to be the one to break it to him, but she had to stick up for her friend.

Ariel said, "Manni give her a chance to explain. I didn't understand it either, but she can tell you what happened. So much has happened since we saw you last. You know, her father died about a month after you left. It was a horrible time for them. And then a few months later her mother died. She was devastated, and I was afraid she had gone mad, but God prevailed, and here you are!" She tried to make light of a huge point.

He looked at her "God prevailed!!!! She is my enemy's concubine!" Ariel said her goodbyes and scurried away. Manni tried to stay calm and remind himself that God had not brought him this far to fail him now. He didn't know what was going on, but he had come for what was his, and by God he would have it. He had heard about her father, and it broke his heart because he had come to love his new father. It was bad enough that he couldn't be there in her time of need, but it was worse to know she suffered the death of both parents and there was nothing he could do. He knew it wasn't his fault, but he felt awful not to be there for her when she needed him most. All he could do was pray! Jesus had told the crowd how to pray. He had seen him again on his way to Samaria; he was in the hillside preaching to a large group of people about the kingdom of God and forgiveness.[64] The words he spoke had touched his heart and renewed his mind of what was truly important. He felt hope for his life again. It was good to see Lamarra again. She looked tired, worn out, and defeated. What was that slimy snake doing to her? He prayed earnestly

---

[64] Matthew 6:14

for his wife, that she would be restored to him and take her rightful place beside him. For he knew he could not live without her. His daughter needed her wisdom to help her grow, to be the woman she would become. He needed her to be his wife, to help him to be a better man and husband.

"God, I believe you ordered our steps and directed our paths to one another. You have a plan for us, and we desire it. Please give me my desire to make my family whole again. Mend the broken hearted and heal the old wounds. Help us to put all the pain and separation behind us, and to have a fresh start together. He camped outside the city with his horse, Azull, determined to get some rest.

Lamarra snatched her arm away from Caleb and screamed at him, "YOU LIAR! YOU DIRTY ROTTEN LIAR! GET OUT OF MY HOUSE!!!" He slammed the door shut.

He said, "Stop yelling like some foolish woman. Let me correct you my sweet...! That would be my house! And I have not lied to you; I told you there was no word on him. We all thought him to be dead in a shipwreck. I can't believe he is alive!" he hissed. Lamarra was fuming mad.

She got in his face, "And I bet you can't believe he spoiled your evil plans to take his possessions for yourself. You lazy adder! I can't believe I allowed you to even touch me. I need to wash your filth away in the Jordan River. I have defiled myself by just being in your presence." She glared at him in disgust. He tried to intimidate her, but she wasn't taking it anymore. Her deliverance was near, and she would break through and breakout of this madness. He threatened her in every way possible, but she wouldn't budge.

She laughed at him and said, "You have no idea what I have suffered at the hands of men! I have been threatened and browbeat by the worst of them. One of them was the most wicked man, I prayed, and my GOD delivered me. I suggest you leave me be for your own sake! I now see what Manni saw in you: a deceitful, lying, evil man. I'm done talking to you. Sleep on the roof and leave me be."

He grabbed her arm and said, "You are my wife and I will have you tonight. It's been three months since I've bedded you, and I will not wait any longer."

"Oh, no you don't! The agreement was when I say so; so get out!" The horse was raging outside and making a ruckus kicking at the door.

She said, "If you touch me I'll scream, and that horse will be in here to defend me. Now let go of my arm!" The horse was getting close to knocking the door down. He let go of her arm.

She said "Calm down, I'm fine, "The horse quieted. Caleb could not believe the horse's behavior. He grabbed his mantle and went outside. The horse snorted when he passed by. Lamarra came to the door and she stroked his head and thanked him for saving her. He was her guardian angel[65]. She thanked the Lord of Host for being her shield and protector. She bolted the door grabbed a knife and went to bed. Her thoughts were only of Manni.

As usual, Manni arose early. It was good to be back in familiar territory. He found the view of the rolling hills and peaks of Samaria peaceful. He poured his heart out unto the Lord and prayed for his will to be done. Whatever He thought was best for his family he would do, but he could not

---

[65] Numbers 22:21-35

promise to be happy about it if it didn't work in his favor.

He packed up and went to the gates of the city. When he arrived, the Elders where taking their place sitting against the wall. People started to gather at the gate. There was tension in the air because this was a sordid spectacle. Ariel was there with her handmaiden to support her friend. She commented on how the chain of events fueled the fire of curiosity; first the Messiah comes to town to save the people; then a wayward scribe's daughter living in sin is judged at the gates! This was an outrage. She could be stoned depending on the law! Manni stood against the wall with his black stallion, looking very dashing in his white turban. His skin was darkened by the sun, and his hair had grown long against his white robes. He was calm and collected, watching and waiting. He was quite a sight amongst the Samaritans; could a daughter of Israel make such an alliance with a son of Ishmael? This will be the talk of the town only second, of course, to the Messiah! How ironic: she that brought the Messiah to the town and now would be judged by his very words.

Ariel's prayer was that mercy would prevail. He patiently waited for the Elders to be seated as Caleb, Lamarra, and the horse walked up. Manni stepped forward when he saw how Caleb was man handling Lamarra. She could do nothing, and she didn't care about anything except seeing his face. She drank in every feature and drowned in his eyes. She had longed to see him, and now she couldn't stop looking at him. He felt the same as he took in the beautiful sight of her. She looked rested this morning, and Caleb looked utterly frustrated! He thought 'that's my girl. Hold him off!' Caleb became more aggravated the more they looked at each other. It almost appeared their love had grown despite the adversity. He hated Manni and everything he stood for. His jealousy fed his envy, which manifested in wrath and bitterness. He would show everyone he was not the nice, humble, honorable man with the spotless reputation that they thought he was[66]! Envy ate at his heart, and wickedness was overtaking him with every evil

---

[66] 2 Chronicles 16:9

thought he had[67]! The Elders were prepared at the Bema seat.

They called everyone to attention. "We are here to discuss the matter of the legal agreement between Lamarra, daughter of Scribe Hosei, and Caleb. In addition, we will address the legal marriage of Lamarra, daughter of Scribe Hosei, to Manehillel of Caesarea of Maritime."

There was a gasp from the people. "She is the mistress of one man, and married to an Arab from Caesarea. Sounds like somebody will be stoned tonight!" Someone stated in the crowd.

The Elders said, "Let the questioning begin. First, let us establish your relationship with Lamarra, Caleb." Caleb stepped forward proud as a peacock, thinking he had already won this battle.

He addressed the Elders and said, "This man named Manehillel attacked my wife yesterday in the marketplace, where I defended her honor in front of many witnesses."

"Thank you, Caleb. That's not what we asked you. What is your relationship to Lamarra,

---

[67] Proverbs 23:7

daughter of Hosei, and do you have any proof to it?"

He started to fidget and said, "When I first came to town, I asked her if I could pay her to provide food and shelter for me while I was here on business. She agreed to the price and she provided meals and lodging for me. I slept on the roof and came down for meals. I asked Lamarra to marry me after helping her with her dying mother. I saw how she needed a husband to comfort her and help her. She had very little support. She wouldn't accept my proposal of marriage. I couldn't understand why she wouldn't; I was taking care of all her needs. She surprised me when she said I will be your concubine and that's it! If that was what she wanted, it was fine with me. I love my wife. You see, I keep calling her my wife because that's what she is to me in my heart. This man is trying to dishonor and take her from me." Lamarra was shaking her head and biting her tongue trying to be quiet. She knew a woman's testimony[68] had more weight if it was witnessed. Caleb accused Manni of trying to conceal his

---

[68] Josephus Antiq. 4:8:15

identity to the Elders by dressing as an Arab to gain sympathy. The Elders could not help to notice how calm and collected he was. They almost thought he didn't understand the language.

They addressed him by asking, "Do you understand our language? And is Manehillel is a Jewish name is it not, or is it Arabic?"

Manni stepped forward and said, "It is Jewish, Elders, just like I am! I am Manehillel, son of Josiah from the house of David. I fully understand the language and speak three others. I know and obey the five books of Moses." Everyone gasped. A Jew in Samaria dressed as an Arab, standing before The Elders, being judged: how intriguing.

"My Elders, I thank you for allowing me to come before you for your wisdom to discern my state. My life, present and future is in your hands and I trust God will prevail in your verdict. My name is Manehillel from Caesarea of Maritime. I am a shepherd and trader. I have known Lamarra for almost 10 years. We met in the marketplace of Joppa where she and her husband owned a shop, and I would purchase wares from them for my wife and household. About one year ago, I saw her in

Joppa and she needed an escort to Samaria. She said she was traveling alone, and I offered to escort her here when we were returning from selling our sheep in Jerusalem. Caleb was one of my hirelings[69] that helped us to get the sheep to market. When we arrived here, she found her father ill, and my men and I helped her in any way we could. She had been a blessing on the journey here, with her excellent cooking and pleasant company. I fell in love with this woman, and before I left Samaria I asked Scribe Hosei to take her as my wife. I was her covering on the trip and afterwards, but I had to return to Caesarea to complete my business."

The Elders asked, "So why are you dressed like an Arab, to trick us?"

Manni said humbly, "There is no deception in me, Elders. When I returned home I was reminded that I was late on another business deal and had to go quickly to conclude it. In order to keep my promise to my bride, I would return for her in one month. But on my way back to Caesarea by sea, I was shipwrecked on Cyprus for over 6 months. I was injured badly and an Arab family took care of

---

[69] Hireling- a worker paid wages, a hired hand.

me. I worked for food and to gain my strength to return home to my bride and my daughter. No one that I loved knew I was alive." He took off his turban and rolled up his sleeves to show the scars from his shipwreck.

"I thought of nothing but returning to my wife and my daughter. With every painful step and breath, I thought of them."

"All of that is very touching Manehillel, and we sympathize with you, but do you have any proof to this?"

Lamarra couldn't hold her peace, "Yes, he does." she shouted. They stopped her from coming forward.

"What is she talking about, Manehillel?"

"Manni explained, "She is referring to our marriage contract that her father and I signed before I left Samaria."

Caleb said, "This is ridiculous. There was no contract between them. I was with him that day. They signed nothing."

With anger raging inside of him, Manni said calmly, "Yes, you were there that day, but when we all walked outside and Ariel came up, Hosei called me back into the house. He told me I had his permission to marry his daughter and we signed the contract. He anointed me with oil and prayed for me." Everyone in the crowd agreed because they knew Scribe Hosei enjoyed baptizing people in oil and praying for them.

They asked, "Did you pay a dowry to Him."

"Yes, Elder I did. 100 silver pieces[70], all of my profits from my sheep and we shared a covenant cup and signed the contract. I also promised gifts to the bride upon my return to complete the dowry."

"So, where is your proof?" asked the Elder.

Lamarra said, "I have it."

"Well, bring it forward," he ordered. Lamarra ran back to the house and got the wrapped skin. She handed it to the Elders. They unrolled the skin and saw Hosei and Miriam's marriage contract, the Deed to their house, and the marriage contract for Manehillel and Lamarra for 100 silver pieces, just as he said.

---

[70] Deuteronomy 22:29, Exodus 22:16-17
Ketubah- contract amount paid in event of divorce, payable by groom at marriage. Jewish prenuptial agreement

Caleb was livid. He yelled, "It's a fake!" He didn't know she had that proof! It didn't matter because she still belonged to him; she was bound by her own words[71]. The Elders perused the document, but only one of them was familiar with Scribe Hosei's signature. It would have been better if they had a document to compare this one with to authenticate it. Three people went to their houses and brought back their documents to be compared with Lamarra's. The Elders ruled it authentic by the other three documents they compared it to.

"So yes, she is the wife of Manehillel, but she entered into an agreement with another man!"

Lamarra trembled like a leaf, because she could hear her father's words, "My daughter, make no vow with your tongue that you cannot keep." She sighed in frustration.

"I pray I won't have to eat those words," she thought. Caleb leered at her like a vulture waiting for his victim to die.

The Elder asked Manni, "Sir, do you still desire to have Lamarra as your wife, even in these present circumstances?"

---

[71] Numbers 30:1-16

171

Manni quickly said, "Yes sir, with all my heart I find no fault[72] in her to reject her as my wife. These circumstances were unforeseen to man but known to only God. The decision she made was under duress without wise counsel. I concede it was my responsibility in forcing her to make that decision. She is righteous in my eyes, sir. I will have her as my bride." He heard a halleluiah shout from the crowd. Lamarra took a breath of relief.

"Not so fast, my sweet," Caleb said. "My Elders, I have purchased the property of Scribe Hosei. So does Lamarra owe me payment for it?"

She said, "You what?" and tried to slap him. "You pig…. You mother of a swine…"

"Lamarra!" Manni calmly called her name and got her attention. The Elder told them to collect themselves before they ended these proceedings. The Elders asked for the papers on the property.

"These papers said you paid off the balance of the loan that was owed on the property. You didn't buy the property itself."

"Yes, but that means I own it right?"

---

[72] Deuteronomy 24:1-4

"No," said the Elders "It means the owner of the property owes you that amount to get their property back. Did you call in the loan and demand payment from the owner in the form of a marriage proposal?"

The Elders said, "We don't understand. Did you or did you not demand payment from the owner."

"Yes, I gave her an ultimatum, either be my wife or be my slave. By rights, I could call in the loan and she couldn't pay, so she would be my slave, right?" Caleb said greedily.

"That is true, sir, but you said this was a marriage proposal- where does that fit in?" the Elder asked.

"I told her for weeks I loved her and wanted to marry her, but she refused. All she said was she loved another and her heart was with him. I didn't care about that, I just wanted her! She would change her mind once we were married,[73]" he said crassly.

---

[73] Deuteronomy 22:28-29

The Elders looked at each other, one of them asked, "So how's that going, has she changed her mind?"

Caleb retorted, "She's with me, isn't she?"

"Not for long," one Elder responded. The man who carried the loan raised his hand. The Elders recognized him as Staymus, and he came forward. He whispered to them and they asked him to speak out loud before everyone. He testified how the Scribe came to him for a loan and how he had paid most of it off after Lamarra had come back, and he vowed to pay off the balance soon. Then about 4 months later, Caleb came in saying he was engaged to Lamarra, and that he wanted to give her a bridal present of the loan being paid off. This would be her dowry and bridal gift to her.

He said, "I was touched because I knew how the scribe had struggled for his family. When I saw how Caleb lived on the roof and they didn't look in love, I asked God to forgive me for trusting Caleb to do right by Lamarra." The Elder asked Lamarra to step forward.

"Lamarra, did you enter into an agreement with Caleb to be his concubine?" they asked.

"Yes, my Elders, I did. I didn't know what else to do. My mother wanted me to marry him because he was following me around like a puppy dog," Caleb bristled at the remark. "But I told her I loved only one man and could not marry another. After five husbands, I was done.

People whispered, "Five husbands… I can't get one!"

"Quiet," the Elders said. "That's the only way women can have security and be safe from being taken advantage of.".

"My heart was with Manni and I made a vow to him, to be his wife forever!" They said the vow at the same time. "And I meant it! I thought the only way to keep my promise to him and survive was to be Caleb's concubine, which is better than being his slave. I thought because he had worked for Manni that he was an honorable man, but that was not true. At this rate, the reputation I had didn't matter without the man I loved. So, I agreed to be his concubine for food and shelter. To live in my father's house and eat food. I offered up my body as a living sacrifice on my terms only, when I said yes, and he agreed to those terms. I know the law, no inheritance[74] and I'm in the street. My Elders, it didn't matter to me because my body was dead, because it didn't have a heart! My heart was with Manni in the bottom of the sea! The Messiah freed me from shame and guilt. For years, I married men for protection and provision; and for years, I was used and manipulated. I saw what true love was in the eyes and heart of the Messiah, he truly cares for us. Manni has shown me that same love."

"The Elders said, "That's wonderful, but did you receive your dowry or any such document saying what was owed toward the loan or paid out?"

"No sir, I didn't," she said.

Caleb said, "I bought all the food, isn't that payment enough?" The Elders reminded him that when you desire a wife or concubine it IS YOUR RESPONSIBILITY to take care of them with the basic necessities of food, shelter, and clothing, without you demanding other favors from them! They were outraged by his insensitivity.

"Did he buy anything for you, Lamarra?"

---

[74] Numbers 27:8

She said, "He hasn't purchased so much as a veil for my face, my Elders."

They said, "We've heard enough. We rule in favor of Manehillel, in spite of the fact that he was supposed to be dead. This influenced his wife's decision, and due to her anguish made a poor judgment under duress. Because he finds no fault in her and is not only willing but desires to have her back, we rule she be returned to her legal husband immediately. Now, the case about this horse!" Lamarra ran over to Manni and jumped in his arms as they shared a passionate kiss. Caleb sneered at their actions. The Elders told everyone to quiet down and to come to order, especially Manni and Lamarra. He held her tightly and away from Caleb.

"Now," the Elders said, "whose horse is this?"

Caleb quickly responded, "It is mine, my Elders. It was given to me to make the journey to see about Lamarra."

The Elder said, "I don't understand, who would give you such a fine animal just to travel to see someone?"

"My Shepherd gave me the horse to come and see about Lamarra and take care of her!" They looked at him like he was crazy. What is this 'shepherds' name?" the Elders asked.

"Johanan, sir," he answered.

Manni managed to get their attention. "My Elders, when I returned to Caesarea I learned that I was delayed in picking up my horses in Tarsus. I had promised Lamarra I would return and the only way to quickly get back to her was to sail there. I took all the men on a ship to Tarsus, including Caleb because he was my hireling at the time. When we got there, I purchased 6 horses. I had to return quickly, so the next day I sailed back to Caesarea and the other men rode back with the horses on land. Johanan is my steward of 6 years and he is faithful. I'm sure he sent Caleb down here to assist my bride in any way, but not marry her!"

"Where does the horse come in?" the Elder asked

"Caleb interrupted, "The horse and I became close on the way home, and I just brought him with me to Samaria."

Manni stepped in with a suggestion, "My Elders, let's end this facade. Let's see whom the horse responds to. Can someone take the horse back to Lamarra's house and do not tie him up. Just stand there with him." They agreed.

"Now each of us will call the horse and see who he will respond to." They took the horse back to the house. Caleb went first.,

"Charger come here!" They waited and waited. He yelled again, the same answer, no horse.

One of the Elders said, "I don't know much about horses, but he hasn't responded. Alright Manehillel call the horse." He went over and leaned against the wall; he released an ear-splitting whistle and called the name Champion. All they heard was the neighing and thundering of hooves. The horse came through the gates and turned to find Manni. He whinnied and trotted over to him. Champion nuzzled him and licked his face. Champion bowed for him to get on and he swung up on the horse. Champion started to walk and prance and change directions without any obvious commands. He stopped and Manni dismounted. Caleb was green with envy.

Manni said to the Elders, "Champion is obviously my horse."

The Elder said, "No, I don't see it that way. I see you are a trainer of horses, and he is one you have trained. Do you have any other proof that you own this horse?"

"Yes sir, I do. First, I have known this horse since he was a foal, and when he was a year old he was gored by a wild boar protecting her piglets. They wanted to put him down, but I said no, let's give him a chance. I nursed him back to health. It took two months to get him on his feet. We have been best friends ever since. If you feel under his right thigh, in the fold, is a scare. Champion, still," he said as the Elder felt for the scar.

"Any other proof, sir?"

Manni said "Yes." his old satchel was truly weathered and stained a person in the crowd caught his eye and he nodded to him. From the inside, he pulled out a smaller purse made from the bladder of an animal. He removed the papers and gave them to the Elders. They announced that these papers proved the sale of four horses, and one white with black mane horse and a white foal were gifts to Manni and his daughter Ilani.

"This is signed by Apollonius, the Greek of Tarsus of Cicilia."

Caleb screamed, "Johanan gave me that horse. He is mine!"

A voice from the crowd said, "May I speak?" Everyone turned to see who spoke.

Lamarra said, "Obadiah!" The Elder asked him to step forward, and he did.

The Elders said, "Who are you and what is your business here?"

Obadiah said, "I am an under shepherd of Manehillel, and I have come with a letter from his steward, Johanan, concerning our master's wife."

"Continue," the Elder said. He gave the letter to the Elder and he read it out loud.

"I, Johanan, steward of Manehillel, give to Lamarra, daughter of Hosei, 30 pieces of silver[75]. This money is to be given to her to use as she sees fit for her benefit, to secure any debt as the wife of Manehillel. I send Caleb, his hireling, with the masters trusted steed, Champion, to deliver this

---

[75] Exodus 21:32: Zechariah 11:12

money to her and he volunteered to go." Caleb was trembling.

Obadiah looked angrily at Caleb and spoke, "We had received word a few days ago that Manehillel was alive and returning home, but he would be getting his wife first. Johanan was upset because Caleb had not returned months ago to give news about Lamarra, or to return the horse. He assumed he had stolen the money and ran off with the horse. We were busy with the harvest, so he decided to wait and possibly go himself. But things were too busy for him to leave. When we got word our master was alive, he sent this letter."

He continued, "My Elders, I was with them on the road from Joppa when we met Lamarra. She was warm and friendly to us. Everyone liked her. Caleb was always trying to impress her. We could see that our master liked her, but he was very honorable to her and protected her always." He glanced at Manni, hoping he hadn't spoken too frankly. Manni nodded his approval. Caleb was assigned master's horse because he requested it, because he had ridden him on the way home.

The Elder said, "Caleb, we have the two witnesses[76] we need to take and put you in prison for being a thief of 30 pieces of silver[77] and the horse called Champion." You are an evil deceiver, and to break the trust of you master, who is paying you to serve him, is a total betrayal; and to steal his wife and manipulate the situation for you advantage."

Another person asked to speak! It was Staymus, the man who carried the loan on Lamarra's house. He came forward with the proof that Caleb had come in to purchase the loan for a dowry to her for their impending wedding, and he had paid 20 pieces of silver.

The crowd erupted, "That thief. Evil scum!" He showed them the purchase papers.

They asked, "Where is the rest of the money, Caleb."

"We have been living off it!" he yelled!

---

[76] Deuteronomy 19:15 two witnesses to convict anyone of a crime
[77] The redemption price paid for a slave. Exodus 21:32; Matthew 26:15

"Put him in chains," the Elders said "and imprison him until he is sentenced. Caleb, you are under arrest for wife, silver and horse thief[78]."

The Elder said, "I don't know this Johanan personally, but he has the same character and integrity as his master, Manehillel. Return the horse called Champion to Manehillel of Caesarea. Manehillel we judge in your favor. You may take your wife and your horse. If you stop by later, we will give you a written decree for your keeping." Manni was shouting praises to God, thanking him." He was so excited God had delivered them all! He thanked the Elders and grabbed Lamarra in his arms. Everyone came rushing over to congratulate them.

Ariel was shouting, "Halleluiah, glory to God!"

The man that had the loan came over to Lamarra and said, "Seeing that Caleb used your money to pay the loan, I will write a new receipt to you and as a wedding present, and in honor of Scribe Hosei will forgo the balance of the loan and your payment will be considered in full." Lamarra

---

[78] Proverbs 6:30-31
Leviticus 6:1-7

hugged the man and praised the lord for his mercy that endured forever. Manni thanked the man for his help and honesty in this matter, and he would look forward to doing business with him in the future. The man smiled and thanked Manni excessively.

Ariel pushed her way forward and hugged Lamarra and said, "Girl, I was about to raise my hand and testify about the kiss I saw at the well between you two," She winked, "but we will keep that between us girls!"

They laughed and Lamarra said, "I do believe all my secrets are out!"

Ariel grabbed Manni and pulled him to her and gave him a big bear hug and said, "Thank you for all you have done for my friend. I love you all and be blessed and prosperous." Manni thanked her but was feeling uncomfortable again.

Ariel laughed and said, "He is so humble!" They broke away from the crowd and ran to her father's house, where they threw out everything of Caleb's and locked the door!

CHAPTER FOURTEEN

This was no dream! When Manni awakened, he felt the warm body of his wife lying beside him. He just took in the moment of awakening with her in his arms. He had waited and longed for this time and he relished in it. She was breathing in his face with a slight snore! Her hair was tousled on his face and her arm was resting on his waist. Her leg was thrown over his and the sheet covering her torso. He loved her acts of possession already! He languished in the faint smell of jasmine in her hair and the blush in her cheeks. He wanted to caress her but allowed her to sleep, for now! His thoughts went to Ilani and how she was fairing. When he arrived in Joppa he sent word to Johanan that he was alive, and to tell Ilani in a few days so he had time to spend with Lamarra. It was wise of him to send Obadiah to Sychar with the letter or we would not have known the depths of Caleb's deception.

"I owe him so much!!! But what am I going to do with these two in my bed! Lamarra and Ilani sleep just alike. This is a good problem to have," he chuckled! Lamarra began to stir and moved closer to him, which caused him to stir as well!

Lamarra's eyes opened in surprise of his physical response and said, "Good morning to you too, my lord!" He pulled her close and blew her hair from his face and kissed her. She wrapped herself around him even more. "What a way to wake up," she thought! They picked up where they had left off in the early morning hours and in total exploration of each other. They enjoyed every moment of their wedded bliss and they snoozed again. Manni's stomach growled and they both laughed.

He nibbled on her lips and shoulder and proceeded downward when Lamarra said, "Let me go so I can feed you properly, my lord!"

He said, "Alright, my love but I will be back for more."

She said, "I'm counting on it!" She wrapped herself in the sheet as she got up. Manni feeling mischievous, held on to the end of the sheet, and as she walked away from him it slid off of her and she was standing in all of her glory with his appreciative eyes caressing her.

She laughed and pulled at the sheet, "Manni let me fix you something to eat."

"I liked what I was already feasting on, my love!"

She quibbled, "Yes, but you have worked very hard and deserve a good meal for your service, my lord," she giggled. He stood up and walked toward her in all his glory and she caught her breath. He was a fine representation of God's creation of man[79]. His muscles were etched on his body and he was lean without an ounce of fat. The numerous scars on his beautiful body would surely tell some outstanding tales. The long scar on the side of his temple gave him a rugged look, but he was still handsome. He pulled her to him and kissed her

---

[79] Genesis 2:25

deeply. His stomach growled again, and they laughed!

"Let me fix some food," she said as she freshened up and slipped on a tunic.

He said, "I will see to the horses," and he freshened up, got dressed, and went outside. Champion was excited to see him and pawed and whined.

Manni hugged his friend and said, thank you for all your help, my friend, but we must be leaving soon! I don't want to rush Lamarra, but I need to see Ilani!" He snorted and pawed the ground.

He said, "Ok, let's go." He tied Azull to Champions saddle and they took off for a ride. The wind in his hair and his trusted steed galloping over the hillside was glorious, all he could do was praise the Lord for blessing him and keeping him; for keeping him alive all this time and for keeping the people he loved safe and secure. He praised the Lord for his word being true and that he had given him the desires of his heart[80]. His heart was free from hurt, pain, rejection, and disappointment. He was free to love again. He had done what Jesus had

---

[80] Psalm 37:4

said: forgave! On his way to Sychar, he did just that, he forgave all the people that hurt him, including Caleb and especially his step-father. He wasn't angry anymore. He felt lighter, free, and happy. He dismounted and allowed the horses to graze as his thoughts went to Ilani. He was sure Johanan had told her my now, and wondered how she reacted. To have lost both parents at a young age is horrible. Fortunately, he would not be going anywhere for quite some time. He would make it up to her and he had the perfect thing. He mounted up and headed back to Lamarra.

The aroma of seared lamb and fresh bread wafted in the air and caused his stomach to growl. He watered the horses and hurried inside. The house was different: pillows were scattered on the rug on the floor, bowls of scent oil burned, a flagon of wine next to a spread of food and fresh fruit was on a platter.

He sighed, "This is what home is like!" He quickly washed up. Lamarra came from the other room dressed in a blue tunic and her hair pulled up on her head with tendrils circling her face. She was a vision of beauty, he couldn't take is eyes off her.

She was so happy. She did not think it possible to feel this way. She had hurried and prepared the house for her husband for his returned. She couldn't wait to find out what his absolute favorite meals were. She was hungry too so she nibbled on some of the fruit. She wished she had more comforts to please him with but that would come with time. She heard him come in and she walked out to greet him.

She said, "Let's eat, my love!"

His stomach growled and he said, "I think I have worked for this meal."

Lamarra gave him a seductive look and said, "You surely have, and you will again!" He nodded in agreement. They sat down on the rug and she fed him choice morsels with her fingers. He ate from her hands and licked her fingers too! He moaned in satisfaction with the meal. She soaked in his love and appreciation for the meal.

When they had finished eating, he pulled her close and said, "Now for something sweet..." and kissed her deeply. She was basking in his love. Tears rolled down her face.

When he released her, she breathed a sigh and said, "I love you, Manehillel, with all my heart and soul. I never want to be without you again!

He told her, "And you never will!" and kissed her passionately. She was swept away by him, his thoughtfulness, care, and concern for everything about her.

He always asked her, "What can I do for you my love?" He aimed to please, to make her happy and to fulfill her slightest desire as his wife. He was a gentle lover and he took great pleasure in pleasing her. He was enraptured with her response to him. Being with her was a new life in love. They slept the rest of the afternoon away. When he had awakened, she was watching him sleep, the love that was in her eyes, she smiled as one caught looking at a dear friend. She inspected his face. His beard was a little scraggly and his hair was long. She kissed the scar along his right temple that stretched to the end of his ear. He searched for her mouth to kiss her again.

He said to her, "I know why it was so easy for Delilah to capture Samson."

She asked, "Who is Samson?"

"We have so much to talk about, my love," he said smiling at her.

She asked, "So how was Ilani when you saw her. I'm sure she was excited to have you back home."

"She hasn't seen me," he said tentatively. She pushed away from him to stand up and stared at him.

"What! You haven't seen her!! Manni that bump on the head has caused you to lose your mind! Does she know you are alive, at least?" He was on his feet backing away from her as she advanced toward him with her hand on her hips.

He said, "I left word in Joppa to tell them I was alive, but to wait a few days before they told Ilani because I wanted to spend some time with you."

"WHAT! THAT BABY STILL THINKS YOU'RE DEAD WHILE YOU'RE IN SYCHAR WITH ME!!!!!" He was getting a little afraid of her now!

He stammered, "My love, I wanted to give you your wedding time[81] without Ilani having to wait

---

[81] Genesis 29:27

193

for me to come home. I also didn't want her to think I chose you over her."

"Well, didn't you?" She said. She was really upset with him for treating Ilani like that.

He said, "So… is this our first fight? Will you forgive me, my love? I was trying to do what was best for everyone. I know my daughter, after thinking I was dead she will not let me out of her sight for a long time; and leaving her to come and get you would scar her again. So, I thought it best to come and get you first, and when we are home, we would not have to leave."

She said, "You bet, you're not leaving us again!" He liked the sound of 'us'.

She said, "I'm sorry, Manni, for yelling at you. I know how my heart was broken when I thought you were dead, and to think poor Ilani all alone without you. I wanted to go to her, but my mom wasn't well, and I didn't think I had any right to her. I didn't know about the marriage papers until Caleb arrived."

He said, "I understand my sweet, but you don't know Ilani. She would be a handful trying to leave her after all that's happened. My peace of mind rested in the Lord and his promises. I was still a little nervous about how things were going to turn out, but I pushed on. I knew Johanan and Sarah were taking good care of her. They have been like family."

"He is a good man, Manni," she said.

"He came to Sychar looking for you after 6 weeks. He hated to have to tell me the news! He was so disheartened not to find you with me. He even gave us some money to help us out. He said he would keep us informed about you, but I never heard anything. Caleb didn't have any news when he came either. I didn't want to believe it, but it looked like I had lost you forever."

"Well you haven't lost me, and I'm here now and forever."

"But Manni," she looked into his eyes and pleaded with him, "can we go home to Ilani? I can't be happy knowing how sad she is waiting for your return." He looked at her with such love and respect.

"My love, I am trying to give you your wedding days before we go home and get busy with everyday life."

She insisted, "Manni she's got to know and see for herself that you are alive! Thank you for considering me, but I can't be at peace knowing that baby is not.

"Well then, it is settled. We leave tomorrow morning." She kissed him deeply.

He said, "Well, maybe we will stay a little longer."

She slapped him on the butt and said, "Get moving Manehillel, we're going home to see our baby.

He said, "I like the sound of that!"

CHAPTER FIFTEEN

There was a flurry of activity as Manni and Lamarra gathered their things. Lamarra knew she would never be back here again so she needed to take everything she wanted. There were a few pieces of her mother's jewelry, Abba's ink horn, and box[82] with his scribe's quills, the great bottle of anointing oil to keep up the family tradition, and Abba's writings on the word of God. He wrote his understanding of the words the priest shared with him. He was always going over his word. This was

---

[82] Ezekiel 9:2

sacred to her because it was the only words from the Torah she would have, and she couldn't come near it as a woman[83].

She asked Manni to prepare it for travel for her, but he felt unworthy of such a task. He prayed before he accepted and asked for God's blessing on him for honoring his father-in-law and his daughter. Abba had taught her a lot about God and she was grateful. She knew that he loved her and answered prayers, just like her father loved her and helped her! There wasn't much to put in order. They decided to take the horses out and then go to the marketplace for supplies for their trip. When they came outside, Azull was pawing the ground, a trick he learned from Champion when they were ready for some exercise. Manni walked over to Champion and told him that they were going to teach Lamarra to ride today and they needed his help. He nodded his head.

Lamarra said, "Champion, you are amazing. Do you really understand what he is saying to you?" and the horse nodded. Manni explained to

---

[83] Leviticus 12; Numbers 8:5-26;
1 Chronicles 23:24-32

her about the reigns and sitting in a saddle. Champion let her get on! The horse bent his knee, Lamarra grabbed the hair on his mane and swung up and sat on his back. As the horse stood up she was amazed at how tall he was.

Manni mounted Azull and said, "Let's go." The horses started to walk. Lamarra was nervous, but Champion was gentle with her. As they got away from the walls of the city, Manni encouraged a gallop. He told her to kick Champion in the sides. When the horse started to gallop, Manni told her to sway with the horse and she did. When they got to the fields, Lamarra kicked Champion and they took off, passing Manni at full speed. They both felt as one with the wind in their face. Lamarra never felt so alive and free. They didn't stop until Champion thought she needed a rest. Manni dismounted and helped Lamarra down, she squealed with excitement.

"I loved it. It was wonderful!"

She went over to Champion and hugged his neck and said, "Oh, you are the best horse, Champion. Thank you for teaching me to ride and for protecting me," she said. The horse snorted and licked her face, and she giggled. Manni asked what she meant by protecting her.

"Oh," she said, "after Caleb punched you in the face at the marketplace, when we got home I threw him out. We… or I was yelling and screaming at him and Caleb started to grab me to make me sleep with him. Champion was outside keeping up a ruckus and he started kicking the door. I told Caleb if he didn't let go of my arm I would scream, and that horse would come in and save me."

Manni said, "What happened."

She continued, "He let go of my arm and he got out. Champion saved me." She rubbed his nose and he nuzzled her making her giggle again.

Manni said, "I do believe he prefers you over me now." The horse whined. They walked in the fields while the horses grazed, and they never felt more alive or in love.

Manni said, "I prayed to God that you would not be given to another man. The only thing that kept me encouraged was you and Ilani, and seeing the two of you again." He pulled her to him and kissed her. Her hands smoothed the tunic going up his back; he was never going to let her go. He fell back on the ground taking her with him and rolled over on top of her. She was crying again.

In sudden caution, he asked, "Are you hurt? Did I hurt you? Is your arm ok?"

He felt her body to make sure she hadn't been harmed, but she stopped him and said, "I am fine, my love. Just overwhelmed with your love for me. I feel like I'm in a dream. No one has ever been concerned for my every move. I love you because you love me so!" He wiped her tears, kissed her lips, and her neck. The horses moved away to give them privacy.

She peered into his handsome face and said, "I'm so sorry for all you suffered for me. When I think that I almost lost you, I can't breathe. I would have no life to live. It was getting hard to exist without you my love." He adored her!

He kissed her teary eyes and said, "Never worry again, my love, for I will never go anywhere without you, because now we are one[84] and I can't be separated from you!"

He kissed her deeply and was getting to know his wife when Lamarra jumped up and said, "We

---

[84] Genesis 2:22

have to go to the market. There is plenty to do before we leave. Let's go Manni." He couldn't believe she left him sitting on the ground. She called for Champion and he trotted right over and bent down for Lamarra to mount him. She had a hand full of hair and swung up on his back.

Manni marveled and said, "You catch on fast."

She said, "Let's go, Manni. We have to get home." He called Azull, who was following Lamarra.

He shook his head and said, "Even the horses are in love with her!" They rode back to the marketplace. A few people were there and congratulated them on their marriage. They stopped at Staymus to get the loan paper. He was very excited to see them. He greeted them and invited them in. He told them that he took the liberty to speak to Caleb about whether he used the money the steward sent to Lamarra in order to pay for the debt. He admitted that he did. In truth, the money should have been Lamarra's, and only 5 silver coins were owed on the loan.

"Your father was highly respected here, Lamarra, and we were all saddened when our brother died. He was my friend too, so I forgive what is owed on that debt. Consider it a wedding gift to you and Manna-hell."

"That's Manehillel, just call me Manni," he interjected.

Staymus said "Here is your decree of your balance paid on the loan, and the deed to the property with your name as the owner." She hugged and kissed the old man and he blushed from all the attention. He made her promise to let him know if she needed anything.

He said, "Begging your pardon. Manna-hell.

That's Mannehillel.... Just call me Manni! Manni replied.

With all due respect to you, just as a friend to her father." Staymus explained.

Manni said, "I understand, and thank you for your kindness."

Lamarra said to Staymus, "I would hate for my parent's house to stand abandoned, could you oversee it for me? Anyone who may be in need of shelter, a widow, a lost soul, allow them to stay there for just a few coins, if any. I will leave that to your discretion. Help our people get back on their feet in their time of need." He bowed and said it would be his pleasure to be of service to her and their people. He wrote up a paper to that fact for both of them.

He hugged her and shook Manni's hand and said, "You are a formidable character as an Arab, you know," and they all laughed. They went to the Elders and got their legal decree concerning Caleb and the trial and went to the marketplace. Ariel and her handmaiden both had big smiles as they waved and laughed. Ariel hugged them both and inquired about what they were up to. Lamarra said they were leaving for Caesarea, and they must come and see them one day. Ariel was strangely smiling and looking at her and Manni.

She slowly reached out and pulled a grassy straw from her hair and said, "A little roll in the hay this afternoon, I see!" She and Manni tried to hide their faces as they blushed from embarrassment.

Ariel kept on teasing them, "You were even scaring the animals. I had to cover my handmaid's eyes," the young girl giggled.

Manni put up a playful defense, "You must have been walking towards us, seeing we were a mile from the road," Ariel laughed heartily.

"You know people are curious about what goes on in the fields when no one is around," she laughed!

"Thank God for Lamarra stopping me, you might have seen more than you wanted!"

"That's what you think," she said and they all laughed. Lamarra hugged her friend, as she battled back tears.

"You never rejected me, and you were always there for me. You encouraged me and defended me to those evil women. I can't thank you enough my friend. I love you and thank you so much. Come visit with us, you and your husband when you are traveling through."

"We will come see you, but we should give you two a little time to cool off," she winked at Manni.

"It's not possible" said Manni and laughed.

Ariel said, "Well I guess I'll have to find some other soul to defend. God's grace and peace be with you both. God bless you and Godspeed." They got their provisions and went back to the house and picked up where they left off in the field.

CHAPTER SIXTEEN

They stopped at the well and filled their water bags. It was a bittersweet moment for Lamarra. She had come home a year ago and buried both of her parents, but found her wonderful husband. Maybe she would return to see Ariel one day. But today was the first day of the rest of her life. The day was beautiful and warm as they made their way through the mountain passes and around the hills. They talked of faraway places that Manni had visited and the things he saw and experienced. Before long, it was time to rest for the night. The horses were tied nearby. Manni gathered wood while Lamarra set up camp. They would need only one palate to sleep on tonight. She cooked a nice meal of lentils and vegetables. The night was perfect under the stars with her husband. As they sat down and ate, she asked, "Tell me more about my daughter." His heart melted when she said, 'my daughter'. He was always worried whether his new wife would accept Ilani as her daughter. He had that same problem with his stepparents, and didn't want that for her. The slightest indication that someone would mistreat her and that's it, they would not be around him or her again. He was very protective of her and she knew it.

He said, "Ilani is the exact image of her mother. She is very pretty to be so young. Her eyes are captivating with those long black lashes. She is very bossy, and that's my fault. I spoiled her rotten and she gets pretty much whatever she wants."

"So, you've made my job even harder, huh?" Lamarra teased.

He said, "When Cassia and the baby died, I was devastated and lost. I was drunk most of the time with a scared child on my hands. One morning, I woke up and Ilani was out of bed. I found her throwing things in the fire pit because she was hungry. I was so ashamed that I was more concerned with my grief than taking care of my child. So, I would get up, feed my daughter, and take her everywhere I went. Like the mothers do, I would tie her to my chest, get on my horse, and do what I had to do. My friend Malachi lived a few miles away and his mother would take care of Ilani when I had to travel. That was normally only with an overnight trip. We were inseparable for a long time. She finally was old enough to play with my neighbor's son, and she was so used to playing rough with him that now I must tell her not to beat him up all the time. Lamarra, she needs a mother to teach her to be a young woman. I'm so glad you're here, and that you want her in your life."

"How could I not want her? She is a part of you, and I love you and I will love her too," Lamarra said with tears in her eyes.

"I don't know what I would have done if Johanan and Sarah had not come along. It was hard taking care of the sheep and farming with a 4-year-old underfoot. Sarah would watch her and prepare our meals, and Johanan and I would work the land.

Ilani always wanted to be wherever I was, and I would put her to work doing something."

"Right, she had to work to eat." Lamarra laughed!

"Well, no," he smirked, "but I felt she needed to know how to take care of herself no matter what would happen. I was afraid for her! She's direct, and adult-like when she speaks, and people are surprised at her behavior. Everyone says she acts just like me! That really makes me scared! A little girl acting like a grown man is not good. That's why she's so bossy. When I'm telling the men what to do next, she thinks she should do the same thing, and when she does, they jokingly obey her but that makes it worse. So, wife, I need your help with our child. I'm sorry I messed things up so bad, but with God's help it can be fixed." Lamarra couldn't wait to meet the small version of Manni. To be a mother was a lifelong dream. She couldn't wait to start her new life. They settled down for the night and they both thought of Ilani.

Manni was up and ready to go when Lamarra finally awakened. She felt drugged by the night air. She looked at Manni and saw the excitement and eagerness to get home. She jumped up apologizing for sleeping.

"He walked over and kissed her lips and said, "Good morning, my love. Freshen up and we can go. I will finish packing up so we can leave." He was always patient with her. She was excited about her new home and she hoped everyone liked her, especially Ilani. She washed up and mounted Champion. Manni asked if she would like to ride Azull and Champion pawed at the ground. They laughed and moved out. They were riding out of the mountain range towards the plains of Sharon. The cool majesty of the mountains suddenly turned to luscious fields of fertile grasslands and marshes further west. It was a beautiful sight to behold. She could see the grazing opportunities in this region. They circled around a ridge and there it was: they could see all of Manni's property unto Malachi and Seth's houses in the distance.

She said to Manni, "Now, that's a farm!" The closer they got, they saw two dots running toward them.

Then he heard her, "Abbbaa, Aaabbbaaa..." Manni took off in a full gallop and stopped short of them and jumped off his horse.

He scooped her up, kissed and hugged her and said, "I love you, baby." Lamarra gave them their time together and beheld the homecoming. Johanan was right behind Ilani. He waited in line to welcome his master home. He was trying to wait his turn, but he had to join in the hugs. Sarah was pulling up the rear with the other workers not far behind.

Ilani was still weeping hard saying, "Abba, you're home. I'll be good. You're home." Manni stopped for a minute to absorb what she was saying.

He looked at her and said, "You are always good, and I'm home baby. Abba's home, ssshhhh." He turned to look for Lamarra and found her staring at Ilani.

Ilani asked, "Who is that, Abba."

He said, "Ilani, this is my wife and your new mother, Lamarra, daughter of scribe Hosei of Samaria." Manni stood up as Ilani had wrapped her legs around his waist and was holding on to his neck for dear life.

"I am so glad to finally meet you. You are a beautiful girl, Ilani. Your father has told me good things about you. You are so pretty; you look so familiar to me. I hope we can be friends." Ilani didn't say anything. She just stared at her.

Manni nudged her and said, "Where are your manners?"

She said flatly, "Welcome to our home, Lamarra."

Lamarra said, "Thank you, Ilani." She looked at everyone else.

She knew Johanan came over and hugged her and said, "Mistress Lamarra, it is good to see you again. You look radiant. This is my wife Sarah."

She said, "Welcome mistress."

Lamarra said, "Just call me Lamarra. I appreciate the mistress part, but I probably won't respond, so please call me Lamarra." Obadiah ran up and hugged them both and they all walked back to the house. Manni could smell the aroma of fresh roasted lamb with onions, garlic, and fresh grilled vegetables. He stepped into his house and praised the Lord for his safe return and keeping his family safe, and asked God to bless his household and everyone in it.

"Everyone praise the Lord, Jehovah Jireh, our provider." They gave a shout for victory. He reached out for Lamarra and kissed her. He went to put Ilani down, but she did not budge, she remained wrapped around her father.

He gave Lamarra a look and Sarah said, "Ilani are you going to show your father his new room?"

She jumped down and ran to his bedroom door and said," Come see, Abba, what we did. It's a surprise!" Manni and Lamarra laughed because the surprise was out now. They walked in to an incredible room.

"It's beautiful." Manni was amazed! The room was larger with a chamber off to the sides. Lamps were burning scented oils with flower petals thrown over the beautiful tapestry covering. There was a side couch with colorful pillows along the wall with stools on the other side. There was a desk in one corner with all of Manni's papers and books and a small ship beautifully decorated. There were rugs on the floor, and a goatskin of long white hair along the side of the bed. Ilani had come to herself and was chattering incessantly describing everything they had done.

"Johanan had done everything you asked while you were gone, and they worked hard to get it done before you got home." Lamarra had not seen anything like it as they entered in the small chamber next to it. They walked through the opening and saw a dressing panel with inlays of beads and small glass window openings on the upper wall that allowed the western light to pour in over the shower area and a tub. The floor was tiled, and the corner had a large basin on the floor with a chair sitting in it, and over-head was a strange container with holes in it. Manni went over and pulled the cord attached to it and water came showering out.

Lamarra was excited and said, "What is it, Manni?"

"It's a shower. My friend has them in his house." There was a large trough with a sheepskin in it full of scented warm water with flowers in it.

Manni said, "For you, my love, to soak your cares away." Tears streamed down her face!

"No one has ever done anything like this for me." She wrapped herself around him and kissed him deeply.

Ilani stood with her arms crossed and said, "Abba, I'm not done!"

Manni said, "Oh, yes you are! I need to freshen up." He bent down to her and said, "Let us freshen up so we can eat."

She sat on his bed and said, "I can sit here and wait for you while you change in that other room." Lamarra and Manni looked at each other. They didn't know what to say! Sarah called Ilani to help her with dinner.

Manni said, "You heard Sarah, go help her. We will be out soon. Can you close the door on your way out, please?"

"Yes, Abba, but I will be back to get you to show you how clean my room is." He escorted her to the door, where Johanan stood waiting for her.

Manni told Johanan "We will be out soon." He closed the door and locked it. He was concerned about Ilani because she was thin and unkempt. He would ask Sarah tomorrow what is going on with her about being "good." He turned his attention to Lamarra.

"My love, how do you like your bath?" He walked in and she was in the tub resting back on the sheepskin, enjoying the luxury. Her body was flushed from the warm water and Manni was tempted to climb in, but he gave her the moment instead.

She sighed, "This is wonderful. I can stay here all day."

"But we can't. Everyone is eager to meet you, and Ilani will not stay away long; the boss will be back as promised."

She laughed and said, "I love her. She is as you said. Her facial expressions are just like yours." He stripped out of his clothes and sat on the chair. Beside the chair was a large vessel of warm water with a large dipper in it.

He poured water on his head and said, "I love to travel, but I hate the dust." There was a small towel he used to clean himself off. He pulled the cord and the cool water showered down on him.

"He shivered and said, "That will wake you up in the morning." He dried himself off and anointed his head with oil. The gentle fragrance of cinnamon was easily detected. She watched him get dressed and knew they would have to talk about all these scars on his body. She was glad her husband was alive. She finally finished her bath and stepped out. Manni was waiting for her with a soft cloth to wrap her in.

She said, "You spoil me." With a smile across her face "You need to be fed, because I'm hungry too," she continued.

There was a knock at the door, "Abba, are you dressed yet? The food is ready. Tell Lamarra to come too!"

They laughed and said, "We are coming." He showed Lamarra to a dressing screen near the opposite corner where tunics hung on hooks for her to choose from.

He said "Here is your table with scent oils for you and comb and brush for your hair. I hope you like them." One was her favorite, Jasmine. She combed it through her hair and put it up on her head. She was beautiful.

Manni slipped in his tunic and said, "Ahh there's no place like home."

He opened the door and said, "My bride, Lamarra." Everyone shouted with joy. The furniture was very unusual at Manni's house. She had never seen a lot of these things before. The eating room had a low table, where they sat on pillows. Manni had her to sit down while Sarah prepared the table with a platter of vegetables and Johanan brought in the roasted lamb still sizzling.

Johanan and Sarah went to leave and Manni said, "Please come and sit with us. We are all family and I would not be alive and with my wife and child if it weren't for you two." They sat down, and proceeded with prayer. Ilani climbed in his lap and reached for a plate and food. They ate until they were full. They talked about their trip down and told the story of how she and Manni met. When Sarah got up to clean, Lamarra offered to help.

Sarah seemed surprised and she said, "You don't have to mistress, I will take care of it."

Lamarra insisted, "I will help Sarah." She leaned close to her and said, "Please, call me Lamarra." Sarah agreed, and they laughed and cleared the table. Johanan was talking with Manni, telling him how excited he was when he got word from Joppa and Tarsus that he was alive.

Manni said, "Tarsus, how did you hear from them?

"Two weeks before a man from Joppa came. A rider from Apollonius came and said they had sailed to Cyprus to find you and heard that you had gotten shipwrecked and was injured. They said that you were healed and now headed to Joppa.

Manni said, "Praise the Lord that Apollo is the greatest friend ever."

"I sent Obadiah with the news and the papers in case there was a problem, because Caleb had not returned." Ilani was still in his lap examining his face and arms, counting the scars on his body. He had to stop her prying eyes.

He said, "What are you looking for, little girl?" and tickled her. She laughed, and the sound filled the house.

Sarah said, "She hasn't laughed since he left." Lamarra's heart broke because for a child not to laugh for a year was unheard of. It showed the depth of her loss and depression. She had the cutest giggle, which made everyone laugh. Johanan was like a kid himself, enjoying his friend. She frowned at Manni and touched a spot on her face and he kissed it repeatedly.

He said, "You know, you have been such a good girl. I have something for you." She squealed with joy and ran to their room. Lamarra ran behind them to see her reaction. She flipped on the bed and did a cartwheel. Lamarra had to move to the side to dodge her feet.

Manni said, "Now, where is it?" She ran to his satchel and opened it up. She started throwing things everywhere. He had to stop her from ransacking his belongings. She pulled out a beautiful cloth rolled around something. She unrolled it and it was a beautiful Arab doll with thick black hair. She had a veil across her face and beautiful big eyes.

Ilani jumped in her father's arms and said, "I love her Abba, she is beautiful".

He said, "When I saw her, she reminded me of you. So, I bought her, so I would have you close to me."

She hugged his neck and said, "I love you Abba, thank you."

Her head popped up and she said, "I know you have more." He pulled out a drawstring purse and she opened it to find two pair of kymbala's finger cymbals. He put them on her fingers and showed her how to use them. He told her how the women on Cyprus, where he was shipwrecked, would dance and have these cymbals on their hands. It was beautiful to see.

He pulled out a beautiful orange cloth and said, Maybe Lamarra can help you make something with this!" Orange was her favorite color and she squealed with joy and flipped on the bed.

Manni said, "Nothing has changed, you are still making a mess of my room little girl. What am I going to do…"?

She said fearfully, "Don't leave, Abba. I'll be good. I'll clean up." She ran around picking up things.

He said so gently, "Ilani, come here sweetie." She came and sat on his lap.

He said, "I want you to know in your head," he pointed to her head and her heart, "that there is nothing you could ever, ever do to make him leave you. I don't care what you have done, you will always be by beautiful daughter, that I love, and I will do anything for you. You see, I came back to you! Now, I was in a shipwreck and I needed time to get well. That's what took me so long to get home. But you are my good girl, and don't forget that."

She grabbed his neck and said, "I love you, Abba."

"Now, show me your clean room." She dropped everything and marched out as they followed her to her little room. Ilani must have about 10 dolls and each one was beautifully dressed and reflected the culture they came from. It was a beautiful collection. Her area was getting too small for her, though. Everyone was settling down for the night. Sarah called Ilani and asked if she wanted to sleep in her bed tonight.

She said, "No I'm going to sleep with Abba, but Lamarra can sleep in my bed if she wants." Manni almost choked.

Lamarra said, "That was generous of her to offer, but I wouldn't be able to fit."

Ilani said, "We gave Abba a bigger bed, so we should be able to fit just fine."

Manni said, "Do I have a say in any of this?"

Lamarra said, "No, you don't." She went in the next room behind the screen to change. Manni was taking off his tunic and Ilani came through the door.

She gasped and said, Abba, what happened to your back?"

He covered up and said, "I've told you about knocking and giving me my privacy. Those scars are from the shipwreck sweetie. Some of them still haven't healed yet. They will get better."

She was crying, "I'm sorry, Abba, that you got hurt. I'm sorry I wasn't there to take care of you." His heart melted.

"Sweetie, God sent people to take care of me, so I could come back to you."

"Abba, I didn't think Yahweh heard me because you didn't come right back, and then I thought I was bad and you didn't want me anymore." He was getting upset with these ideas she had. Where she was getting these thoughts. He hugged her and said, "Stop worrying sweetie. I love you and it will never change or stop me from getting to you." Lamarra watched them with tears streaming down her face. They all piled into the bed together Lamarra to his left and Ilani curved in his arm on the right. Maybe tonight everyone could get a good night's sleep.

CHAPTER SEVENTEEN

He got up and got on the couch, but it was no use, they slept like wild cats. So he left them to fight for space. This last month he had been kicked, punched, scratched, slapped, and kneed in the groin. He decided it was enough to make a grown man cry! He thought all his pain was over after the shipwreck, but this was insane. No sooner than he had moved, they jockeyed for position for more territory. He just laid there, watching them sleep. He was worried about Ilani and this whole talk about being "good," so he was reluctant to leave. He had to find out what was going on. He also had to find a way to get her in her own bed because he was missing his wife.

Ilani had gotten taller, but she had also gotten skinnier. She had dark circles under her eyes. She didn't look well. Is this what is meant by the phrase "worried sick"? He needed time to talk to Lamarra, because she looked at her in a peculiar way and he couldn't get a private moment with her. Ilani monopolized her father's time from morning till night like she was his shadow. She went everywhere with him, whether he was with Johanan or not. She was not letting him out of her sight. At night, she climbed right in bed, and if he was attentive to Lamarra, she would interrupt him. She demanded his attention and got it. Manni tried to sneak and put her in her bed after she fell asleep, but she would awaken, screaming for him. He couldn't believe she was acting like a 3-year-old all over again. He got up off the couch and went to get some coffee. Johanan was stirring too. After a restless night, he asked his friend to be seated, and allow him to serve him.

He said, "I learned to pray while you were away!"

Manni looked at him and said, "I'm glad," not understanding what he was really saying.

He said, "Master; I couldn't bear not having my master and my friend around. It was hard to stay strong for Ilani when she asked when you were coming home. I didn't know what to do or say. I sent messengers to Tarsus and Joppa hoping to hear news to no avail. Ilani wouldn't eat or sleep. She stayed in your room. Sarah had to go in there and wash her up and try to revive her, but she was depressed and loss. We don't have children, so we didn't know what to do. Sometimes she would eat a few bites and drink a little water. When she started to get a fever, we were scared. Sarah had to get tough with her and tell her, 'Manni would be upset to find her sick when he came home' and that she had to look her best when you came home. She started to perk up a little, but every day, she would go outside and look to the ridge to see if you were coming home. She started to lose hope. We asked Seth to send Samuel to visit her more often. It was interesting to see children handle adult problems. Samuel came in here and asked her how she was, and she barely said two words to him. He told her to help her dad keep the land up while he was gone. He told her 'I don't think your Abba is dead, but all I know is you got to keep going until you know for sure. You got to get up and get busy taking care of you father's business.' She got up out of bed and she started moving around more, but it was hard to get her cleaned up. It was a fight every day. Sarah wanted to wash her hair and she only let her wash it once. Another time, she just poured water on her." Manni served them his favorite Arabic coffee, and Lamarra came out.

He said, "Would you like some?"

She responded, "Yes."

Johanan smiled at her and said, "I couldn't tell her I saw Lamarra and you weren't there. That was my last hope that you were with your bride."

Lamarra sipped the coffee and said, "What is this…" and almost spit it out.

Manni chuckled and said, "It puts hair on your chest, according to Sarah."

She said, "No, thank you."

Manni asked, "She keeps telling me that she will be good, so I don't have to go. What is that about? He was trying to make sense of a nine-year-old's pain.

Johanan said, "I noticed it too! We don't know how she came up with that. We'll go get the horse today." Lamarra started bustling in the kitchen when Sarah came out.

"Sorry I slept late."

Lamarra said, "I'm glad. Now, you can rest for a change. I refuse for you to get sick waiting on adults who can do for themselves! I need you for other things...like girl time," she said and winked at Sarah.

Sarah just looked at her confused and said, "What time?"

Lamarra laughed and said, "Have a seat, I'm cooking this morning and you, my dear, will sit and enjoy. You're looking tired." Manni threw up his hands.

"We've got another boss in the house. I guess we better get out the way, Johanan." They went to the barn and left the women to the kitchen. Lamarra made some tea for them and added a dollop of honey to it.

Sarah took a sip and said, "This is good. Thank you, my mistress... I mean Lamarra."

She said, "You are welcomed, Sarah. I want to thank you for taking care of my family all these years. That could not have been easy. Manni eats like a horse and Ilani is a handful! You have done a great job, and you make it easy for me to come into my new home. Everything is neat, clean, and orderly. It's like you are a sister to me." Sarah was speechless. She didn't know why her mistress was talking like this. Lamarra saw the confused look on her face and explained.

"Sarah, I was an only child and I had few friends. It's nice to have another woman in the house to talk to and help with the chores. You are not my slave or steward, I consider you my sister. I hope that is pleasing to you because it is to me."

Sarah said, "What is girl time? It is time we set aside to talk and do what we do: fix each other's hair, make things and talk?" Making sense of what it was, Sarah said, "So, it's a lot of talking while we do things."

"Yes," Lamarra exclaimed, but it didn't sound so exciting the way she said it.

She added, "We spend time together without the men or children, but I think we will include Ilani to help her move in the right direction." Sarah nodded and said she was willing. Lamarra was rustling up a meal and checking the spices and supplies. She was impressed at the selection and freshness. She asked her where she got her herbs. She told her she would show her the areas to find them in the market in Caesarea. The Romans there had a good market of spices and wares from Asia and Greece. They were there when ships came in to disperse their wares to the Roman consul and things shipped to Egypt as well.

"We would take Ilani with us to port hoping it would brighten her day, but she would come back depressed because Abba wasn't there. She would look at the face of every man looking for Master. She would come home and jump in Manni's bed and cry herself to sleep. I would go in to comfort her and she would push me away. She would roll herself in Manni's clothes and bedding and not come out for hours. Fortunately, Johanan was able to coax her out most of the time to take her with him to do things. He told her he wasn't sure how her father would want him to do something and she would have to go and tell him what to do, but when she finished she wanted to go back to his room. Obadiah and the other men caught on to the game and needed her advice on everything every day. They told her she was doing a great job taking care of Manni's farm while he was gone. She responded to Johanan more than me. She wanted her father. One night she woke up screaming for Abba and Johanan ran in the room and picked her up in his big arms and brought her to our bed. She clung to him and wouldn't let go. He sat on the side of the bed and rocked her to sleep. When I woke up the next day, she was lying across his chest, still clutching his clothes. I've never seen a child so sad before. Johanan was able to get her to eat a little, but it was never enough." Lamarra went into the bedroom. Ilani was still sleeping. She was a beauty to behold but a dirty one. They would try to settle that today. The smell of fresh bread followed her into the room. She kissed her cheek and forehead and smoothed back her head and called her name gently. She kept calling her name and Ilani's eyes fluttered as she looked around and saw Lamarra. She rolled her eyes and turned over.

She said, "I cooked something special for you Ilani, and I think you should freshen up before Manni and Johanan eat everything up."

She sat up, "Where is Abba?"

"He's out back in the barn with Johanan." She promptly got out of bed and marched to the door.

Lamarra said, "Ilani, come here for a minute."

She walked over to her and said, "Yes?"

"Let's fix your hair a little," she wiped her face and she dabbed some fragrant oil on her hair and neck. She said, "Now, go say good morning to Abba and tell him to come eat." She walked pass Sarah and grumbled a good morning and Sarah replied. They watched her go outside. A few minutes later, everyone was at the table. Ilani had her seat on Abba's lap and Lamarra served Manni and Johanan first then Ilani and Sarah and then herself. Everyone devoured the food; even Ilani was eating all her food.

Manni kept sniffing Ilani saying, "You smell good enough to eat." She giggled and looked at

Lamarra. Lamarra smiled and they all sat and talked about their plans for the day.

Lamarra mentioned, "We will have some girl time this morning and see what Ilani wants to do with that beautiful fabric she has." Ilani's eyes perked up!

Manni said, "I will be out back in the barn cleaning it out for the harvest.

Lamarra said, "I'll heat the water for you for when you come in." They cleared the kitchen and went to Ilani's room.

Lamarra said, "Now, where is that lovely fabric." She had a box at the side of the bed and she had all the fabrics Abba had purchased for her. Lamarra looked through them and found several that she had picked out for him.

She said, "These are lovely, Ilani. Your Abba loves you so much he always provides for you." She held the fabric up to her and said, "This would look beautiful on you. Abba would love it." She agreed. She continued, "When Abba see's you in this he is going to hug and kiss you, So, we better get you cleaned up. You know Abba always freshens up before he plays with you." She looked surprised as she remembered.

She said, "What should I do, Lamarra?" Lamarra's heart melted at the fact that she asked her something for the first time, and that meant the world to her.

She said, "How would you like to take a bath?" Sarah and Lamarra poured the heated water in the tub to a nice level for her and placed a sheepskin in the bottom for her to sit on. Lamarra had her dunk her head in the water too and she rinsed her hair repeatedly. She smoothed in some olive oil and ashes soap[85] that were in a small container and rinsed her hair. Lamarra hummed a song her mother had taught her. Ilani asked her what she was singing, and she said it was a song about the goodness of God. She scrubbed the little one down and plucked her out of the tub. She pulled out the plug in the corner and the water ran out into a drain in the floor. Lamarra marveled at all the nice conveniences in her home. She wrapped Ilani up and sat her on a stool, where Sarah joined them with cups of tea. The aroma of sage swirled inside

---

[85] Soap- Jeremiah 2:22

of the cup. They talked about girl stuff, like the pretty clothes they saw on the Roman women in port and the beautiful furniture. The jewelry they saw shine like the sun on the consul's wife. Ilani just sat their taking it all in. She drank her tea and told Sarah to get her some more.

Lamarra leaned over to her ear and said, "Ask her nicely."

Ilani said, "I'm sorry, Sarah" Can you get me some more tea, please?" Sarah was stunned.

She said, "Of course, mistress." Ilani looked up at Lamarra and she winked and nodded her head. She released a small smile. She combed her Jasmine oil in her hair and brushed the waves together. She loosely braided her hair to keep it together while it dried. She went to her room and found a clean tunic to wear.

It was a little short, but she put it on her and said, "We have to make you some new clothes little girl, you are growing up!" She kissed her cheeks and Ilani got a whiff of the scent Lamarra had on.

She said, "What flower is that that you are wearing?" She told her it was Jasmine and ginger mixed together.

Ilani said, "May I try it?" She put a few drops behind her ears and put her sandals on her feet.

She said, "I'm going to show Abba!"

Lamarra said, "Wait, let me wrap your hair."

She stopped and asked "Why, Lamarra?"

She said, "We just got you cleaned up and your hair is still wet. Let's wrap your head in your veil to keep the dust out, so it will smell fresh." She allowed her to wrap her head in her veil. She took the brass mirror off the shelf and showed Ilani how pretty she was, and she went running to her father.

Lamarra could hear Manni saying, "Who is this vision of a beautiful little girl." Ilani squealed with glee. Her laughter was heard all over the farm. Sarah and Lamarra smiled and nodded to one another and now worked on themselves. Lamarra was trying out the shower when Manni came in. She had placed the panel in front before she sat down.

He walked over and scooped her up and kissed her passionately, and then he whispered softly, "Thank you, my love."

She said, "You, my love, are always welcome!"

He started to peruse her body when Ilani busted threw the door, "Abba! Where's Lamarra!"

They both said, "Go back out and knock." She turned around and went back out. Manni came out of the bath chamber.

She knocked on the door and he said, "Come in."

"Abba, where's Lamarra? My veil fell off and she has to put it back on."

She answered, "I'm in the shower, Ilani. I'll be out in a moment, just wait for me in there." Manni's plans were foiled again by the little one, but he was just glad to see her clean! She looked better today, not so tired. Lamarra came out of the shower wrapped in a towel and Manni changed his plans for the day with one look. Lamarra winked at him.

He pulled her to him and kissed her and said, "Thank you," and he sniffed her neck until she giggled and pushed him away.

"Go with Johanan so I can get dressed."

Ilani said, "Abba, this is girl time!" Lamarra bucked her eyes and looked at him "... scram, its girl time!"

He obeyed and mumbled, "I'll be glad when it's my time."

Lamarra said, "I heard that!" Lamarra let Ilani comb her hair for her and taught her how to smooth the oil thru it. She asked her about her friend Samuel.

She said, "Do you really beat him up?"

She said, "No, he lets me win. I beat him running and everything, so I let him win when we're wrestling."

Lamarra said, "Well, you are a pretty girl. You really should leave the wrestling to the boys. Lamarra rubbed her Jasmine scented oil on her skin and Ilani rubbed her back. She slipped into her tunic behind the dressing screen and fluffed her hair and twisted it on top of her head. She went outside to find Manni and he saw his two lovely girls and sighed that angels were walking on earth.

Ilani asked, "Where?" as she looked around. They laughed. Johanan smiled with approval and disappeared.

Manni grabbed Lamarra, kissed her, and said, "I love you."

He picked up Ilani and said, "You are growing like the cedars of Lebanon. I must get you some new clothes and shoes."

She said, "Abba, I want some jasmine oil like Lamarra."

He said, "Next time I go to port, we will have to get some."

She clapped and said, "Yesss. Where are we going now, Abba?"

"To Uncle Malachi's."

"Are we selling something for him?" she asked.

"No, we have to pick something up, and we can show Lamarra the land."

She said, "Come on, Lamarra, don't forget your veil, your hair is still wet." Manni laughed as Lamarra ran and got her veil. They got the horse out of the barn and Azull walked over to Lamarra and nuzzled her.

Manni laughed and said, "I know who you will be riding today." Champion nodded and nuzzled Manni.

He told the horse, "Now that you're tired of my wife, you will settle for me." The horse nodded, nuzzled, and sniffed Ilani.

She pushed his nose away and said, "Don't, Champion. I'm clean today." Everyone laughed and mounted to go to Malachi's. Ilani chattered the entire ride. Manni kept looking at Lamarra and rolled his eyes. He hoped she would join in and save him, but she let them have their moment. She kept thinking about Ilani her beautiful eyes and the brown color of her skin. She had seen them before. It's as if she knew her already. She just starred at her. Ilani jumped down from Manni's lap and ran to Malachi's door and knocked. His steward answered the door and asked her to come in.

She said, Thank you Amos. Is my uncle in?"

"He is around back with the horses." She turned around and said, "Abba he's with the horses." They were talking to Ester. She saw them coming and had come around to greet them. Ilani just stood there watching her. She hugged Manni and then gave Lamarra a little hug.

She said, "Oh, come in for a moment before you go back there." They walk into the beautiful courtyard. Lamarra sighed with wonder.

"It is beautiful, Ester!"

She said, "Thank you, it is my father's house, but my brother and I live here."

She said, "Congratulations on your marriage. May God bless your union. You caught the best prize in Caesarea, Lamarra."

Lamarra said, "Yes, he is the best prize and I'm truly fortunate for him to be mine." They walked into the spacious home. It was like a roman home on the inside large spacious rooms with water and closets. The furnishings were roman-like as well, with the exception of one room being strictly Arabian. She was amazed at the beauty and colors everywhere.

Malachi walked from the rear of the house and said, "I was waiting for you all. Is that my honeycomb, Ilani? Look at you, you have grown!" She jumped in his arms.

"Yes, I have and Lamarra washed my hair today and wrapped it so it wouldn't get dirty."

He said, "You smell delicious," and tickled her.

Ester said, "I'm glad, because you were a little pig running around." Lamarra shot her a look that could kill. Ilani rolled her eyes. Manni watched Lamarra.

Malachi said, "I see why you have kept your beautiful wife away from me, Manni. I would be tempted to steal her away from you." Giving Lamarra his attention, "Mistress you are truly a vision of loveliness. I see why my brother had to return to you, he was truly your captive."

She blushed and said, "I was the one captivated by his love!" as she looked at him lovingly. Manni was hoping she could read his mind right now!!

Malachi said, "Well, I think someone is nine-years-old and deserves a present to celebrate. What a good girl she had been while her father was away."

Ilani squealed with excitement, "What is it uncle Malachi? What do you have for me?"

He said, "Come with me." They all walked out to the back. There was a huge stable behind the house with caretakers for the horses.

Lamarra asked, "Who are you people?"

Malachi laughed and said, "We are just hard-working traders, that is all." He spoke to two men and they ran back into the stable and one returned with a little saddle.

Malachi presented it to Ilani and said, "This is for you, from me." It was heavy, so he held it for her.

Manni said, "This is from me for you being such a good girl all the time, especially while I was away. I love you Ilani." The man brought out a beautiful white horse with a black mane, just like champion. She caught her breath, "Abba, for me?"

"Yes, baby for you," he said. He brought the horse closer to her and she rubbed his nose. He sniffed her hair and nuzzled her. She laughed with excitement. They put the blanket and saddle on the horse and walked him around. Manni instructed her on how to handle the horse and how to talk to him and stand near him. He whistled for Champion, who came around from the front with Azull behind him. When Champion recognized his foal, he pranced.

He said, "Let's go for a short ride." Malachi picked up Ilani and put her on the horse. Manni swung up on Champion and rode side by side with Ilani. She was thrilled to have her own horse.

As they went for a ride, Malachi suggested, "Let's go in for a drink," and Lamarra and Ester followed him in the house.

Lamarra said, "Your house is magnificent. I have never seen such beautiful things."

Malachi said, "My father was a merchant and went all over the world to purchase wares. He would travel with Manni and me so we could help him bring things back. We were on a ship at twelve-years old. Manni quickly picked up on the languages, and Father used him to translate when trading. He also caught the travel fever. He should have been a sailor because he loves the sea. Anyway, everywhere we visited, my father brought something back to remember the place by. When we went to Rome, it was beautiful. Unfortunately, after a few disappointing events one year, we never went back. We set our fortunes on other places. I have continued to collect beautiful things, but nothing as beautiful as you. My brother has made an excellent choice in you, and I hear you can cook too! If it is one thing my brother loves to do is eat!!!!

Yes," they both said, "he works to eat." They heard them returning. Lamarra went to the veranda and Ester was standing next to her.

She said, "He spoils her too much. That is that girl's problem. She will never behave getting everything she wants."

Lamarra ignored her and said, "I'm sure he knows how to raise his own child."

"What does he know, he's a man? This girl will be running wild by next year."

Lamarra turned and said to her, "I doubt it. Now that I'm here we will work together to help our daughter."

Ester said, "Your daughter, that little Bedouin. She needs to learn some manners." Lamarra stiffened at the remark and was getting angry and chose to run and catch up with Manni and Ilani.

She asked, "How you do like your horse, sweetie?

She gushed, "I love him, Lamarra."

She said, "You will have to think of a name for him." Manni thanked Malachi for everything and whistled for Azull. Lamarra mounted the horse and they went home. Ilani talked to her horse all the way home.

CHAPTER EIGHTEEN

Lamarra handed Manni the reigns and gave him and Ilani time alone with her new horse. She was angry, but was putting together the pieces of her memory. She walked in the kitchen and saw Sarah was beginning preparation for dinner. She told Sarah to have a seat, which she did willingly.

She said, "Let me fix you some tea."

Lamarra looked at Sarah and asked, "When is the baby due?

A bit puzzled, Sarah said "What baby?"

Lamarra said, "You are with child, you know!" Sarah was shocked. She didn't even know!

"I... I... didn't know what was wrong with me. I thought I was just sick."

Lamarra said, "How long have you been throwing up and can't stand the smell of Jasmine?"

Sarah said, "How did you know?"

Lamarra said, "Because you ran out of the room when Ilani and I were getting dressed and combing my hair." Sarah rubbed her stomach in amazement.

"Mistress, I never thought I would see this day. It's been a long time coming." She started to cry and Lamarra comforted her with a hug.

"You'll find yourself crying a lot, and sometimes for no reason at all. It's part of being with child. You must tell Johanan, he will be excited to be a father. He was a good one to Ilani when Manni was gone, so he will be even better with his own." Sarah was still amazed. Lamarra got busy fixing the dinner. Manni and Ilani came in laughing and joking.

"Lamarra, guess what I named the horse." Ilani said.

"What did you name him?"

"I'm going to call him Shekel, like Abba's name is about money."

Lamarra said, "That's a trader's daughter for you."

Ilani asked, "Sarah, what can I do for you? Are you sad."

She said, "No, I'm not sad. I'm just tired."

Ilani responded, "You go lay down. Lamarra, and I will take care of dinner." Manni's head snapped around and looked at Lamarra who was, strangely enough, looking up at the ceiling and anything else not to burst in laughter. Ilani started giving instructions.

"Abba, go freshen up and let uncle Johanan know Sarah is tired." Manni suggested that she go freshen up as well, before she helped with dinner.

She giggled and said, "Yes, Abba." and ran in his room to clean up.

Manni kissed Lamarra, "You are a miracle worker."

She said, "No, God is!"

Turning his attention to Sarah, He asked, "Sarah, are you alright?"

She said, "Yes master... Manni, just a little tired."

He said, "Go lay down and we will help Lamarra with dinner." She looked at Lamarra and she nodded her head as she starred at Manni.

"You will help with dinner?"

He stuttered, "Uh, yea. If you need me too!"

She said, "Lord, you are working miracles today!"

When Ilani came into the kitchen, Lamarra asked her where was her veil. She said Shekel had snorted all over it sniffing her head.

She said, "That's ok. Come on in and help me." She taught her how to shell peas and to cut up cucumber. The kitchen was a hub of activity and delicious smells and sounds. Ilani was humming a song when Manni came out of the bedroom and leaned against the wall and watched his women in the kitchen. He loved having his family together at last.

He asked Ilani, "What are you humming?"

She said, "A song that Lamarra taught me about the goodness of God." He loved this woman so much!

"She has a pretty voice. I have to teach her words, so she can sing for us," Lamarra stated as she got the figs and apples and citrus fruit and some spices. She asked Ilani to come and help her, which she did in obedience. She told her they were going to make a favorite treat of hers for Abba that reminded her of her friend. She had a bowl and a spoon in front of her and had her measure the flour in her hand, then poured in the oil to make the dough. She showed her how to chop the figs, nuts, and apples. She added the spices and the citrus juice. She rolled a ball of dough in her hand and patted it flat and put a spoonful of fruit mixture in the dough and sealed it shut. She placed them on a pan and set them aside. They placed the food on the table and told everyone to come eat. The food was delightful as usual, but Sarah was still a little queasy. Johanan looked worried and Lamarra encouraged him to go attend to his wife. Assuring him she and Manni had everything under control; he hurried into the room and closed the door. Manni took Lamarra in his arms and kissed her and thanked her for her kindness to them.

She said, "Sarah is my sister and I love her and appreciate all she has done for you and Ilani. We must take care of her, because she took care of us."

He kissed her again and said, "Let me help you, my love." Manni helped clean up the kitchen. He wasn't a stranger to it, but it had been a while since he had to do it. He was blessed to have Sarah cooking for him and Ilani. He looked around and Ilani was gone. He looked in her room and she wasn't there either. He checked his room and found her sitting on the couch playing with her new doll. He was glad to see her happy and clean!! Lamarra called her from the kitchen. She just sat there in bliss.

Manni said, "Did you hear Lamarra call you, Ilani?"

"Yes, Abba," she said and went in the kitchen and said to Lamarra, "What can I do for you, Lamarra?" She was her father's child. She even said it the same way he did.

"Yes, help me finish these treats for Abba."

"Anything for Abba," she said!

Lamarra started to say, "You know, Ilani I took one look at you and saw how beautiful you are, but

I keep thinking that I know you from somewhere. You are only nine-years-old, and I never met you before until now. It has puzzled me until now." She took the treat out of the fire and sat them on the table to cool. She took the honey off the shelf and grabbed a spoon. She had Ilani drizzle the honey over the warm cakes and she waited. She got a cloth and put two cakes on them. She called Ilani over and whispered in her ear. Manni suspected they were up to something with him.

Ilani came to him and said, "A treat for my sweet," and fed him a treat. The cinnamon and citrus and sweet taste of honey melted in his mouth.

He said, "Oh baby, that's good."

She said, "Thank you, Abba. She tasted her handy work and said, "That's good, Lamarra. May I have another one."

"Sure sweetie." Lamarra said to her, "When I was a little girl I would go to the well with my mother to get water."

Manni took a seat He wanted to hear this.

"One day when we were there, a caravan came up. The women came over and said 'hello' and asked if they could get water. We said yes, they could. I saw a girl about my age peaking around her mother's skirts. I smiled at her. I walked toward her and waved. She waved back. Our mothers looked at each other and approved of our playing while they drew water from the well. The little girl had long thick lashes. She was beautiful even as a child." Ilani looked up at Lamarra and said, "Who was she?" Lamarra continued her story. "We played together that whole harvest, and then they moved on. She had given me a doll when she left, and I gave her my veil. We were sisters. I loved her and still miss her to this day. My friends name was Kezia. She was the daughter of a Bedouin Sheikh. Her name means Cassia, which is the spice called cinnamon." Ilani started shaking and crying. Manni was shocked and could not speak. Lamarra bent down and looked her in the eyes and said. "I know I have stared at you some days, and I'm sorry Ilani. I was trying to remember why you looked so familiar. Manni is right, you look just like your mother, but you have your father's lips his smile. Your mother was my childhood friend and I'm so glad I'm with you I feel I have Kezia back with me through you."

"You were friends with my mother?"

"Yes, baby" she said. She looked at Manni. He confirmed that Kezia[86] was her name but she went by Cassia, the spice, which is cinnamon and her father, was a Bedouin Sheikh. He had traded with Manni for years and Manni saved his life in the market place from thieves. He offered him his daughter in marriage in gratitude for saving his life. When he gave her to wed and she took off that veil, it was love at first sight. She was beautiful. She was a jewel of a wife. She was smart, vibrant, a great cook and the love of his life. Lamarra hugged her. Ilani hugged Lamarra as they both cried. Lamarra picked her up and she wrapped her legs around her. Manni went to take her and Lamarra shook her head no. She carried her to Manni's bed and they climbed in. She snuggled with Ilani and sang a Child's lullaby to her. It took Manni back to his childhood. He realized this is what Ilani had been robbed of with her mother's death. The thief

---

[86] Kezia- Keziah- means cassia or cinnamon.
Job 42:14 Jobs second daughter

had robbed her of a mother's comfort and love during bad times. He covered his girls and left them alone.

He went outside and walked and thanked God for his wonderful wife, who loved his daughter as her own and took the time to win her heart. He thanked Cassia for sending her friend to him, a continuation of the love he had with her. He was a blessed man. He thanked the Lord for his goodness and mercy to him and his family and he would serve him always. The prophet was right, there was healing coming to his house. He walked into the bedroom and they were wrapped in each other's arms. The Lord just kept answering prayers. He had survived being shipwrecked to get his wife from another man. He brought her to his land of plenty and to his daughter who needed a mother. He stretched out on the couch and watched them sleep. They both lazily opened their eyes at him and said, "I love you" and went to sleep.

Lamarra woke up not able to close her mouth because Ilani had her hand in it. Her foot was in her pelvis and she felt like she was holding her down so she couldn't get up. She slid from under Ilani and she rolled over and continued to sleep. She wiped her face and brushed her hair in place. She went in the kitchen and the men were having their morning "hairy" coffee as if they didn't have enough hair on their chest. She knew it was their way of saying it was strong only for men.

She walked over to Manni and said, "Good Morning, my love," and bent down and kissed him. She apologized to Johanan for the public display, but she couldn't resist, he was so handsome in the morning light.

Johanan said, "It's your house. I've got work to do," and he started to leave.

Lamarra stopped him laughing, "How is my sister, this morning?" she asked. Johanan loved her calling Sarah her sister.

He smiled and said, "She's fine, and expecting a child," he beamed.

She said, "Congratulations, Abba." He was so excited.

"There is so much to do, with the harvest and the celebration and now a baby coming."

Manni said, "Don't worry, we will get it all done. I'm happy for you my friend." Sarah called him. He took her a cup of tea.

Lamarra sat down and said, "Ouch, my ribs hurt."

He said, "I know that feeling. Ilani is a rough sleeper; I got the better end of the deal last night. I slept like a baby."

She sighed and said, "God will deliver us, my love. We shall be free to love again."

He said, "Yea, some Manni time." She giggled and Ilani was up with her hair standing all over her head.

Manni screamed and said, "What is it? The hairy girl is attacking us!" Jokes at her expense first thing in the morning, was not funny to her.

Lamarra chuckled and said, "Sweetie, go get my brush for me." She stumbled back into the room and got the brush and climbed in Lamarra's lap. Manni just watched the transformation. Lamarra continued to talk with Manni about the things they needed to do to prepare for the harvest. Manni talked about how he wanted to celebrate their marriage at harvest time, and invite everyone to join them. That maybe their friends could come and celebrate with them. She thought it was a great idea, but she wondered where everyone would sleep. She said that most of them were good Jews and would practice the Feast of Booths or Sukkoth. But his friend Apollo did everything big. He would probably bring his own house down from Tarsus.

She said, "I would love to see that!" He said how he would be working with Johanan on the fair end of the property building a house for their guest, and he would ask Seth if some guest could stay at his house during the festivities. They would go to the port to see if some supplies came in.

Ilani asked Lamarra, "Can we go for a ride today?" She looked at Manni and he nodded.

She said "Sure." Manni asked her to ask Malachi if Apollo and his bunch could stay with him or take in some guests of ours.

She said, "Sure I will ask him." Ilani was pretty with her hair combed and braided in two rows. Lamarra rustled up some food for everyone and checked on Sarah. She said she would be up later this afternoon to pick some fruit from the garden.

As they rode over to Malachi's, they saw Samuel walking along with his slingshot.

She said, "Lamarra, can I go see Samuel?"

She said, "Yes, but meet me at Malachi's so I can finally meet him."

"Yes, Lamarra." The horse kneeled to let her dismount and Lamarra took the horse with her. She dismounted Azull and tied them to the post and knocked on the door. The steward invited her in the courtyard. It was a beautiful space.

Ester came out to meet her and said, "Good morning, Lamarra. What brings you to us this morning?"

She said, "I wanted to talk to Malachi about the harvest festivities."

"He in the back with the horses," she said.

"I'll wait for him out back." She decided to walk around and get the horses, that way Ilani would know where she was. As she got closer she overheard Ester yelling at Samuel and Ilani. She told him to quit throwing rocks around her and to go home and do that and to take the little goat herder with him.[87]

---

[87] Song of Solomon 1:5-6

Ilani said, "I'm going to tell Abba you are a mean woman!"

"I don't care what you tell your father. I need to slap your little dirty face, you Bedouin," and she raised her hand.

Lamarra screamed "DON'T YOU DARE TOUCH MY DAUGHTER!" She walked up to Ester and poked her in the chest with her finger and pushed her backwards. "Don't you ever in life talk to my daughter like that, do you understand me? I will take a stick to you myself! You are the one with no manners." She grabbed Ilani and pulled her behind her.

"If you so much as look at her funny, I will do something you will regret. Now tell these children you are sorry, before I beat you myself." Ester tried to get away from her, but she grabbed her clothes. Malachi saw and heard the whole thing and was laughing under his breath. Someone needed to get his sister, and Lamarra was just the person. Lamarra told her if she didn't apologize she would start breaking every bone in her body. Malachi walked up, and Ester ran to him saying Lamarra was crazy. He responded by telling her that she was crazy for messing with Lamarra and Ilani, and she better apologize now. She did so reluctantly, and ran in the house. Malachi apologized for his sister's behavior.

"Unfortunately, she thinks she's better than everybody because of her wealth. She really wanted to marry Manni, but he thought of her as a sister. She forgot why she came, and mentioned the harvest festival to celebrate their marriage. They walked back to the house because Lamarra needed to calm down. Samuel was staring at her with his mouth open. She finally noticed him.

She said, "I'm sorry Samuel for you to see me act that way."

He said, "I think you're the greatest mom ever. Ilani your mom is a warrior. She's the greatest. It's nice to meet you Lamarra. I got to get home and tell my dad I met you. Wow what a mom." Lamarra felt awful. Now everyone would think she's a crazy woman. She sat down to talk to Ilani.

She said, "Sweetie, she had no right to talk to you like that, she was wrong."

Ilani said, "Why does she call me a bad one. Samuel was throwing the rock, not me, but I'm the bad one. I wasn't bad, and Abba said he would never leave me. She said he was tired of me being a bad one and that's why he left, to get away from me." Lamarra wanted to go and beat her into the ground. Ilani didn't know it, but Ester was referring to her being a Bedouin not a bad one. She decided it was best not to explain it now.

She said, "You let me know if she says anything else to you. She can only say 'Good morning' or 'Good bye' and that's it, or I will beat the skin off her back!"

"Like Abba's?" she said.

She said "What?"

"That's what happened to Abba when they would travel. When he was young, the men beat the skin off his back."

Lamarra hugged her and said, "No sweetie, I would never do that. I'm just angry for her talking to you like that."

She said, "Lamarra, am I really your daughter?"

She said, "Yes, sweetie. I married your father and that makes you my daughter," she opened her arms and said, "Will you have me?"

"Yes, Lamarra."

She pulled her in her arms and hugged and kissed her and said, "Let's go home and check on Sarah."

While they put the horses in the barn Ilani asked "Lamarra, can I call you mama, now that I'm your daughter?"

Lamarra said, "I've been waiting for you to say it!"

"Thank you, mama, for protecting me, I love you." They both cried and went to check on Sarah. They found her out in the garden picking herbs and fruit. Lamarra and Ilani grabbed a basket and joined her. Ilani ran ahead to pick her favorite fruit and Sarah and Lamarra talked. She asked how she was feeling. She told her it was better in the afternoon. She drank some tea and ate some bread. She was still amazed she was pregnant because they had given up all hope. She said she was afraid to get close to Ilani because she was her master and how could she be her mom as her slave. She wanted to mother her so many times but knew it was out of place.

Lamarra said, "Not anymore, auntie. No slaves around here!" She asked how did Johanan become

Manni's slave because he doesn't even think like that, Ester I can see, but not Manni.

Sarah looked at her, and said, "You noticed." She told her story.

"We met Manni on our way to Jericho, from Jerusalem. We had stayed a bit to talk to a friend. When I went to relieve myself, a few men robbed Johanan. When they found me in the woods, they took me, and then tried to sell me in Jericho. Manni had found Johanan on the road and helped him to a person's house that agreed to take care of him. When he got to Jericho he saw me on the slave block and purchased me. He asked for papers from the men who were selling me, and they had none, so they would release me because Manni was not my husband claiming me. He purchased me and took me to Johanan and signed the papers over to him and gave our host some money and went on his way. When Johanan was well, he looked for Manni for months and vowed to pay him the debt owed for purchasing me and paying for our stay. It was a difficult time for Manni because his wife had died, and he was too proud to ask for help. He finally let us on to help on the farm. Johanan was a big help to him. Manni was so good at trading goods that he always had something to sell. He was always going back and forth somewhere. We looked out for Ilani while he was gone. At first only Malachi's mother would take care of her, until she died. Then he left her with us, sometimes overnight. My husband loves Manni; he loves working with him, his business sense and most of all his integrity. Manni is greatly honored wherever he goes. They love him in Joppa and Tarsus and in Jerusalem."

Lamarra said, "They love him in Samaria too!"

"Well when Manni told him he had paid his debt and he was free to go, he refused to leave him because he was his friend and he loved him.

Manni jokingly said, "So you want me to nail your ear to a post, and Johanan said "Yes!"

"What," Lamarra said.

"Yes, Manni hated himself but Johanan loved it, he was stuck with him for life. He loves your husband more that anyone. When he didn't know whether he was dead or alive, he searched for him and sent the men out to find him. He was crazy about finding him. He needed confirmation that he was dead. Attending to Ilani helped. It was a distraction for him, but he was in the fields taking care of business every day until he came back."

Lamarra said, "I'm sure you want your own life, not tied to someone else."

"Mistress... Lamarra, understand me when I say we love Manni, you, and Ilani, but I can't help but want my own home. That's where we were headed that day, to buy some land and start our lives together and got robbed, but thank God for Manni. The two of them have built an empire on this farm and Malachi and Seth are part of the family too. They all grew up together and stay together to help each other out. Manni is the salesman; Malachi has the connection even though Manni has his own; and Seth is the agricultural wisdom he tells them what crops to grow and harvest and plant. They have been doing this for years. Johanan always wants to be connected to this house and knows he's not blood, so he has to be a bond slave. Manni doesn't like it but he puts up with it. "Manni met them in the garden when they finished the other storage house, and asked if

Ilani wanted to go to port with him and Johanan to see the ships.

She looked at Lamarra and said, "Mama, do you want me to go with Abba." Manni couldn't believe his ears, she called her mama!

She said, "Sweetie, you can go with Manni if you want to. The decision is yours."

She looked at Manni and then at Lamarra and said, Abba, I'm going to stay here with mama, because we are going to have dinner ready when you come back, and mama needs my help because auntie Isn't feeling well." They all stood there shocked!

Manni said, "Alright then, I will see you all when we get back."

She said, "See you later, Abba." Lamarra called Manni back and pointed to a spot on her cheek and he kissed it and her lips and kissed Ilani too! She said to the ladies never let them leave without your kiss on their lips. The women took the food in the house to prepare dinner.

CHAPTER NINETEEN

It was a busy time around the farm; everyone was working on some area of the property. Today, Manni had everyone come out to the new building they had put up. When the ships came to port a few weeks ago, Johanan and Manni went down with carts and mules to bring back all sorts of things. They took them straight to the storage house. Today they all rode the horses to the new house. Sarah didn't like riding, so Johanan rode with her. Her baby bump was showing now. They all stood outside the house and Malachi, Ester, Seth, and his wife, and Samuel and all their workers stood around. Manni faced them all and was very nervous. Lamarra smiled and nodded to him. He told everyone that Johanan was one of the most important people in his life. He had come into his life at the darkest time and let his light in. He had been the greatest help to him over the past seven years[88] and he is his best friend.

He said, "When I was injured in Cyprus, he took care of my family, property and business. I want to let everyone know today, that while I was away, Johanan did not take his rightful share of the profits from this farm as he should have and that was a substantial amount. I've been going over the books since I've returned and found that he did not even take his share of food and provisions that he had already labored for on this property. So I bring you all to witness my gift to Johanan, for his service to me, and my family as my Steward." He walked up to Johanan and removed the slave ring from his ear.

"You, your wife, and family are free. I relinquish your bond service to me. I know why you wanted it done, but I would have your child

---

[88] Exodus 21:2-6

born free[89]. These are the papers stating your freedom. Also in these papers, if you desire to be my Steward for a fee, we will make arrangements for a percentage of the profits." Johanan had tears running down his rugged face.

He said, "You two have taken care of me and Ilani for years and even my new wife, but it's time for you to take care of yourselves in your own home." Sarah griped Johanan's arm. Manni said go into your new house. Sarah opened the door and they entered in their home. Johanan embraced Manni and Lamarra and thanked them. He had been setting up his own home. He thought Manni was building it for his friend Apollo to stay in during the harvest and wedding celebration. Sarah and Lamarra walked through the house. It had several rooms and they were large with plenty of space. The storage area was large as well.

He told Johanan, "Here are your property rights. You sit on 3 acres of land near Seth and me. He even put a shower room in their bedroom. It was perfect. Sarah went into the bedroom and

---

[89] Exodus 21:2-5

there was a small cradle for the baby. Sarah was still shocked.

She hugged Lamarra and said, "Thank you so much. This is a dream come true. I love everything. You and master are so generous."

Johanan said, "I hope you like it. We have to put a sheepskin and combed wool to soften it for him." Johanan and Sarah thanked Manni and Lamarra as everyone walked through and blessed them with a gift. Johanan took Manni outside, away from the crowd.

He said, "Mast... Manni, I cannot thank you enough for my freedom, my home and my life. I owe it all to you."

Manni said, "No, you owe it all to God. We have reaped where we have sown[90]. I helped you and you helped me. God put us together, so we could help each other. I pray for you and your family as if they were mine."

Johanan said, "I do too! So, we are, from now on, brothers, family and partners forever. If you decide to move on, we will miss you but understand the need to live your own lives not

---

[90] Galatians 6:7

obligated to anyone else. We love you. Enjoy your new life."

Sarah said, "We will be back tonight to prepare dinner". Manni and Lamarra looked at each other and shook their heads.

Ilani said, "Auntie Sarah, you do not have to do that for us anymore. Mama and I will cook for Abba. You just take care of uncle Johanan, he eats like a horse like, Abba."

She said, "Yes. Mistress... I mean my lovely niece, Ilani. Only if you promise to come and see me, and of course help me when the baby comes."

"Oh yesss, auntie. I would love to help!" Everyone slowly returned to their homes to give them privacy. Lamarra was talking to Malachi, Johanan and Manni seemed unable to part.

Malachi said, "Lamarra, this could only happen now that you are here. Those two were inseparable, but now that Manni has you, they will be fine. You are good for him!"

She said, He is the best thing that has ever happened to me. I thank God for him and Ilani every day."

She asked, "Were you able to contact everyone for the celebration?"

"Yes," he said, "All the messengers returned with everyone responding to your invitation. Even Apollo has extended his hand in all this." She was excited and couldn't wait for the event. They walked back home with the horses in hand and talked of Johanan and Sarah's surprise. They put the horses away and finished preparing the storage areas for the harvest. Ilani and Lamarra went in to freshen up and prepare dinner. Ilani was chopping all the vegetables and asked Lamarra to teach her the words of the song her mother taught her. She began to sing about the goodness of God, and all he's done for me. They sung it together and Ilani's voice was as captivating as her eyes. Manni stood watching them in the kitchen. His family was complete. He hoped that all the pain that they had experienced would melt away with their love. That the new life they had would be full of the goodness of God and his blessings. Lamarra looked up and saw Manni looking at them. She smiled and winked at him.

Ilani saw her looking at him and said, "Abba, when are you and mama going to have a baby, like Sarah?"

Manni stared at Lamarra and said, "I don't know sweetie. We have been very busy since we got home. We don't have time to work on that. We must get the harvest in and then the celebration. We have a lot to do. Tomorrow is a big day; we start to harvest the barley and then the wheat. The first fruits of the harvest we will give to the temple and then we will fill are storage bins. Get your rest tonight." After cleaning up after dinner, Ilani and Lamarra went in her room. She tried on a tunic Lamarra had made for her of orange and blue fabric, and she found a dark blue sash to wrap around her waist. She showed off her new shoes and pranced in front of Abba with her new outfit.

He said, "You are beautiful sweetheart. Mama did a good job on your tunic."

She said, "Samuel says she is the best mother!"

He asked, "How does Samuel know she's the best mother?"

She said, "Because mama was going to beat up Esther for calling me a bad one." She said, "I threw

277

the rock, but Samuel did too, and mama came from the back and told her she better leave me alone, and not to speak to me again. Mama said she would break every bone in her body if she touched her daughter. That's me, Abba."

Samuel said, "I told you Esther was evil. She and Caleb were always plotting against people, especially you, Abba. But mama told her not to say my name or touch me ever!"

Lamarra looked sheepish and said, "I was so mad, Manni."

He held her in his arms and said, "Thank you for defending our daughter." He kissed her, and they looked for Ilani. They went in their bedroom and shower room, and she wasn't there. Lamarra said, "Manni, she was asleep in her bed." Manni went to freshen up and Lamarra took Ilani's new clothes off. She stirred a little. She put on a tunic for her to sleep in.

She said, "Mama?"

Lamarra said, "Yes sweetie."

Ilani said sleepily, "I love you and I'm so glad you're my mother, and Samuel is too!"

She kissed her forehead and cheeks and said, "let's not forget our prayers." Manni stood outside listening to them pray. His heart was full of love for this woman that had changed his life. His hair was still wet from the shower and he was still wrapped in a cloth when Lamarra walked in.

He looked behind her for Ilani and asked, "Where is she?"

She closed the door and said, "In her room and in her bed." His eyes bulged as he said, "Really now?"

She bolted the door and said, "Really!" They had not been together since Samaria. He knew that look. She untied her hair and walked to him and wrapped herself around him. He caught his breath as he brought her close and kissed her like it was the first time. She melted in his arms. He loved her response to him. Every muscle in her body said, 'I love you.' He caressed her and lifted her to their bed.

Manni said, "What can I do for you, my love?"

She said, "You have done it all. All my prayers have been answered. I hope… I hope I have pleased you. I am so happy, I love you, my daughter, my home and my life."

Manni said, "Pleased me....? Woman you are my rib. God designed you especially for me. As we lay here, our hearts beat as one. He fashioned every curve and tilt of your head, soft lips, and wonderful hands for me. And he designed me for you, to love, provide, protect, and take care of. I've been searching for you all my life and for forgiveness, acceptance, and peace and I have all of that with you, my love. You are more woman that any man could want and I'm grateful that you are my wife and have accepted my daughter as yours. I love you and can't ask for anything more."

They demonstrated their love to each other and were in each other's arms all night. Manni knew his wife Lamarra and they slept until the morning light. They slept late into the morning. They couldn't believe how much room was in the bed without Ilani. Manni slumbered and Lamarra got up and freshened up while he slept. She tipped toed out the room and went in the kitchen. There was Ilani trying to fix a meal. She had treats on her mind. There was flour all over the table and fruit and nuts everywhere.

She chuckled and said, "Would you like some help? What are preparing for us to eat, my love?"

She said, "Mama, how do you make this look so easy."

"You will get the hang of it. Do you need some help?"

"Yes, I wanted to surprise Abba. I want to make the Cassia cakes."

She said, "We will, but I think your father will want more than that to eat!"

"But mama, we don't have to cook a lot of food because Johanan and Sarah aren't here anymore."

She said," Oh, yes we do have to cook a lot of food because Manni can eat a camel on his own. Let's get the beans and rice and vegetables going. You chop, and I'll get everything else going." Ilani started to sing the song Lamarra taught her and she looked up and Manni was standing in the doorway watching them. They looked at each other and smiled.

Ilani said, "Good morning, Abba," and smiled at him and looked at Lamarra and smiled at her.

He said, "What is that look for? Don't I get a hug and kiss this morning?" She ran and jumped in his arms and kissed and hugged him. He had flour all over him, even in his hair.

She said, "Abba, I beat you up this morning. Your time with mama must have made you sleepy." Lamarra turned her back so they wouldn't see her laughing.

Manni said, "It does make me sleepy and I slept really good!" He smirked.

"Did you sleep well in your bed?"

"Yes, I did, Abba. You were not in my way. I could turn over and stretch out. I know you missed me sleeping with you, but I have more room in my bed. I think I will sleep there unless you need me to keep you company."

"No, no your mama is there to keep me company if that's ok with you Ilani. You can sleep in your bed!"

"That's fine, mama belongs in there with you."

"Yes, she does," he said with a lecherous look on his face.

She forced a stern look on her face to stop from laughing and said, "Manehillel we have work to do this morning, getting the harvest started and sending in our first fruits. You need to get dressed so we can get started."

"Yes Mistress, Lamarra," he said as he bowed to her and got dressed. Ilani laughed at Lamarra and Manni's playfulness. They sat down and Manni blessed the food and they ate heartily. He told them to meet him in the barn. They finished cleaning and cooking the Cassia cakes and wrapped their veils around their hair and joined him in the barn. They got the mules out and strapped the carts to them and led them to the field. Johanan and the other men joined in harvesting[91] the crop. They started with the barley harvest and stacked the bundles in the cart and took them back to the threshing floor. While Manni was threshing, they picked fruit and vegetables from the garden. They were to clear the barley fields and the garden of fruits and they gave a portion to the temple. They continued working well into the evening. When they came in from the fields, Lamarra prepared food and everyone went to shower. Ilani

---

[91] First fruits – Exodus 23:16 Exodus 34:22

beat them in the shower and when she pulled the cord she squealed due to the cool water.

Manni said, "I was wondering where you ran off to. Invigorating, isn't it."

She said, "I like mama's bath better. It's warmer than the shower." This was their routine for the next two months and all were tired but satisfied to get the harvest of all that they needed. Now they had to prepare for the wedding celebration!

CHAPTER TWENTY

She traced the scars on his back with her fingers. She thought so many times what he suffered for her! She kissed the large scar down the side of his back that had gashes of exposed muscle where the skin had never covered it. There where old lash marks, as if he had been whipped. All these things he didn't talk about and he never complained of. He stirred and mumbled a warning that if she keeps waking him up like that, they will never leave this bed.

He rolled over and said, "Good morning, my love. You're curious this morning."

She asked, "Manni, what happened on Cyprus? You've never said a word about what happened to you."

"My love, I didn't want to speak of these things with Ilani present," he replied. "She already tried to peek under my clothes to see my back when she felt the ridges and bumps."

"I feel it is my fault you went through all of that. Had you not come back for me and forgot about me...," she began

He interrupted her, "I would be a most miserable man," he said. "Which I was!"

He cupped her face in his hands and kissed her and pulled her close "Don't you ever blame yourself for what happened to me. It was nobody's fault. If it was anyone's fault it was my own. I was so anxious to get back to you that I didn't listen to Apollo[92] when he said the weather was not good that day for sailing. I should have waited, but I didn't, and he was right. The ship got caught in a storm. It is in the winter that the weather starts to get too bad to travel, and it came a little early that year. Anyway, I was shipwreck and I remember

---

[92] Wise counsel- Proverbs 11:14 and 15:22

swimming towards a beam that was on the water bobbing with the waves. When I reached for it, it hit me in the face and I blacked out. But God was gracious to me.

When I awoke, I was floating, attached to the beam by my satchel that was hooked on it. An Arab family pulled me out and took care of me. They said I didn't wake up for a few days and I had four broken ribs. The beam was shattered, and it ripped at my skin when it carried me along. It was a small price to pay for being alive and to have you as my wife. It was so hard to breathe, and it hurt so badly. The gashes in my face and back were excruciating, and they changed the dressing frequently and applied a salve to it. They wrapped my chest tight, so I could heal, but it took a long time. I thought of you and Ilani, wondering what had happened to me or thinking I was dead. I was blessed of God because my legs and arms were not broken. I got a fever on one occasion, but it broke, and I got better. I wanted to get a message back to Tarsus to tell someone I was alive, but the weather was bad for sailing in the November and December months. So, no one was traveling from Tarsus those months. No other ships came in, and I was miles from the port I was sailing to. No one knew where I was, not even me. I spoke a little Arabic. So I was able to communicate a little, but they spoke a different dialect. The sheikh's daughter spoke Arabic and communicated with me for them only when necessary. I knew how protective they were of their women, so I stayed away and looked away whenever they were around. After a couple of weeks, I could move around a little better and tried to help care for myself. The women would not allow me to ruin their hard work.

I slept near the horses' stable and that's where I met Azull. He was my companion. He encouraged me to move around by bumping me to get up and he would help me. I started taking care of him, brushing him and next I was training him to kneel and prance and walk on his hind legs. The sheikh was impressed and asked me to train his men to train the horses and I did. One day he was trading some of his horses and I told one of the men to tell him the horse he was buying had an injury. He told me to prove it and when I pushed on that area of the horse's body he reared up and moved away from me. The sheikh appreciated my skills, so I had to work for my food. I traded his horses and even minerals and copper from the region.

When I was ready to leave, I had earned some money for myself, as well as increased his wealth greatly. He tried to give me one of his daughters, but I declined, and I told him I respected him and my wife too much. He blessed me, and we said we would see each other again. I had to get to the other side of the island to get a ship to Joppa that took horses on board. When I got to Joppa, I was so excited because I wasn't far from you. After only a day and a half ride, you would be in my arms. When I arrived, my friends told me that Johanan had been looking for me and they thought me dead. So, I sent a message to him from and Joppa and went to Sychar for you, my love. When I was in the market and saw Caleb touching you, I could have cut his hand off, but I kept hearing Jesus preaching being good to your neighbor and forgiving people what they do to you. I was conflicted until he put his hand on your hip. All I remembered was you are my wife! When I was a young man, Malachi's father took us to Rome, and I helped a roman official's wife carry the things she had purchased from us at the market. She stumbled when we were walking, and I went to help her and grabbed her breast accidently. Her husband saw the whole thing, but he accused me of taking liberties with his wife and had me flogged."

"Oh Manni, I so sorry for your pain." He said, "Baby it is over now. But know that your love is the best healing medicine I have. So just keep loving me Lamarra. Today, we are celebrating our marriage with all our friends and family so let's get ready."

They jumped up and filled the tubs and showered with warm water. The grounds were all prepared for the festivities. They built a veranda on the front of their house and had raised a tent for Apollo's family a few days ago. Many of the guests were arriving already. Malachi and Seth were hosting for some of their friends. Seth had Manni's friend Simone, the tanner, and Dorcas and her friend staying with him and his wife. While Ariel, her husband, and her handmaiden had stayed with Malachi because (Ariel could handle Esther.) Apollo and Adonia arrived a few days earlier. They had arrived at port and everyone was amazed at how they traveled. They had plenty of stewards and helpers of all kinds. They had the best of everything but gave to anyone they saw. It was not uncommon for them to give a piece of jewelry or a piece of clothing to anyone on the street to be a blessing. They came loaded down with all their provisions for their family. The children were running up to the house looking for Ilani, screaming her name. She ran outside to meet her "cousins" she had never seen. They had heard so much about each other. They went to run and play, and their squeals and laughter made the house come alive. Manni and Lamarra stepped out to greet their guests. She was stunned to see the beauty and statuesque of Apollo and Adonia- this is what Greek gods looked like. They were stunning. Apollo walked up and kissed Manni and Adonia likewise. He had told her of their kissing people they considered family and they came right over and kissed her on the lips too! She stared at Adonia for she never saw a more beautiful woman, and Apollo could make one's heart stop he was so handsome. They came in the house and Manni showed him to his room to reside in Apollo appreciated the hospitality, but he said, "You know brother, I am ready to raise the roof wherever I am."

His men were already outside raising the tent; it was bigger than Manni's house. All the comforts of home were with them. It was a spectacle, and everyone came out to see them raise the tent. Apollo and Adonia teased Manni about getting his wife. Adonia said, "I even tried to fix him up with one of my sisters and he would not even look at her."

Lamarra said, "He didn't know it then, but those eyes were for me only."

Lamarra didn't know that Apollo and Adonia knew about Manni's ordeal in Rome that's why Adonia pressed him to be himself and not hide. But she did notice that this time when she kissed him he kissed her back, and she smiled at him and he at her because, his confidence was back as a husband. He wasn't afraid of misconceptions because he had a beautiful wife and one who loved to kiss him as well as family of friends[93]. They watched how

---

[93] Holy kiss- Romans 16:16; 1 Thessalonians 5:26

quickly they put the tent up and how majestic it was. As soon as it was up, the children proceed to run through all the curtains and walls. Apollo and Adonia just laughed and chased the children in and out of the tent. They were bigger kids than the children. Manni got dressed in Johanan's old room. He had cut his hair months ago at Lamarra's request. He agreed that he was the priest of the house and should trim his hair[94]. He wrapped a small turban of white linen around his head with a white and gold tunic that he purchased in Tarsus long ago. He added an over mantle with it, and he had new shoes he paired with his signet ring and dress rings. He had his bracelets as well. He was a handsome site to behold. He waited for his bride. When she came out, she adorned for her King in that tunic which draped her body with a sash that hugged her waist even tighter. The orange and blue tunic and mantle were stunning in design and she wore two veils. They both were shear: one blue and one orange. She had necklaces on that were beautiful and bangles and bracelets.

---

[94] Leviticus 19:27 Ezekiel 44:20

He said, "I want to give you your bridal gift before we go out."

She opened a wooden box inside was a lovely fabric and she uncovered her jewelry from Manni. Inside was a bridal veil of copper with lapis stones and gold coins in it. There were matching earrings and a necklace with cooper metal and blue lapis stones inlayed with gold coins dispersed throughout. It was beautiful craftsmanship.

Lamarra said, "Ohhh, my love, it is beautiful!" Her hands were shaking.

"Let me, my love." He helped to fasten it on her. He placed her jeweled headdress on and the jewels settled right over her eyes that brought attention to the lovely brown eyes. And then he put on her necklace and earrings. She was a lovely vision of complete beauty, and she thanked him so.

He said, "You are always welcome, my love." She kissed him, and he said, "Let's go see our guests."

Everyone was seated on cushions and couches to enjoy the festivities. When they came out of the house, everyone shouted for joy and praised the name of the Lord. They sat in their places as king and queen of this event. Manni first welcomed his entire guests from near and far to celebrate his union with Lamarra, daughter of Scribe Hosei of Samaria. Then, this union was joined together by God who had ordered their steps and directed their paths to each other- that every prayer had been answered for them in each other. They had made a covenant of marriage over a year ago and an adversary tried to keep them apart, but it was not to be. They persevered in the Lord and obtained their prizes of each other.

"She is a wonderful wife, more than what I could ask for, and a great mother to my daughter who Ilani loves with all her heart. Please enjoy yourselves and all we have to offer." The music began, and they began to eat. Many people came up to the couple and gave them gifts and blessed them and their union. There was one of the workers with a person on a mule.

He helped her down and as she walked over to them, Lamarra's eyes lit up and cried, "Mother Tirzah!"[95]. It was the old widow woman that she lived with in Joppa. She extended her arms to the

---

[95] Numbers 27: all

295

daughter that she loved and welcomed her in her embrace.

She said, "Mother, how did you get here, how did you know?"

"Manni had sent a man to Joppa to invite those that knew you. He saw you waving to me when you left Joppa and figured you two were close and it would be a great surprise for the celebration." And it truly was a surprise. She sat mother next to her and Manni hugged her and called her mother. Apollo's children entertained everyone with their tumbling abilities and gymnastics. Ilani had come forward and beautifully sang a song to Manni and Lamarra about the Goodness of God. She had dressed Ilani in the outfit she had made for her of the favorite orange material with the light blue sash and veil. She was a lovely vision.

They talked with their guests and danced together. When they sat down to rest a moment, Lamarra called Obadiah over. The men brought a trunk and sat in front of Manni. Lamarra stood up and honored her husband. That he was one the greatest gifts God had given her. He was her protector, provider, priest, husband, and lover. She thanked God for him every day. She wanted to give him something special because of her great love for him. He was surprised at her gifts. He rose and opened the trunk, and the first thing he pulled out was a new satchel. Reddish brown leather with plenty of compartments and a small waterproof pouch for papers and imported articles. It was a great idea because the old one was blood stained and denatured from the salt water. That satchel had saved his life with the help of the Lord. But it was time for a new one. The next item was a cobalt blue mantle with white stars of David woven in. It had silver clasp on it with a generous hood. It had been stored in cinnamon and had the perfect scent, with blue leather shoes to match it. Manni was overwhelmed; he loved his mantle that Dorcas had made for him. She made it so he would not forget! His grandmother and father were Jewish, and his mother was a Samaritan. So many people in Joppa considered him a half-breed, but in Judaism one is the nationality of his or her father[96]. Some people treated him differently in Joppa, so he moved away with his young bride, Cassia, to the outside of

---

[96] Genesis 48: all Halakha- jewish religious laws

297

Joppa. Dorcas missed having him around to sell her wares. The mantle was beautiful with full pockets, compartments, and attachments on the inside of it as well. He kissed her, for he had lost the other one in the shipwreck. When he sailed, he always put his cloak on last so if he had to shed it quickly, his satchel and knives would not be in the way. He appreciated the old mantle even more after Lamarra had taken to it and wrapped herself in it to stay warm. She told him there was more, and he pulled out the horse's swags and tassels for the reigns[97] of Champion and Azull. In the bottom was a small box and in it was a beautiful ring made of turquoise and silver. He was overwhelmed. No one had ever given him such thoughtful gifts. The things he wanted to replace, she knew what they were. And to think of his horses was amazing. In the bottom, was a gift for Ilani. Manni called her over. Ilani opened the box and it was turquoise jewelry. There was a necklace, a nose ring, and an earring. There were two rows of turquoise and silver to adorn her face[98].

---

[97] Judges 8:21
[98] Song of Solomon 1:10

She yelled, "Mama, I love it! It is so pretty!" Lamarra put them on her face from her nose to her ear.

She hugged Lamarra and said, "Thank you, mama. I love you." Ilani and Manni kissed Lamarra and asked her to stand up.

Manni told her how much he loved her and never wanted to be parted from her, and Malachi brought out Champion's mare.

She was white with a black mane. She pranced and walked and nodded to Lamarra, who asked, "When did you get her?"

Manni told her, "Malachi has had her for you all this time. I wanted her to be your surprise wedding present."

She replied, "She is beautiful, Manni! I love her. Her name is Magnificent! That's beautiful, but I will add to her name mercy. I will call her Magnificent Mercy! God has been magnificent to us, and I thank him for his mercy.

Manni said, "I have one more gift,"

She sighed. "My love, you overwhelm me with your generosity and love what more could you give?"

He pulled out a small box. When she opened it, she wept! In it were two rings that were connected when placed together. One was hers and the other was Manni's. It was two rubies[99] rings set in gold that when fitted together made one ring.

He said, "My love, I am not complete without you and I can only be whole with you[100]! Thank you for loving my daughter and me and making us yours. I will always love you and cherish you forever!" Lamarra was crying and the widow, Tirzah, was blotting her tears and praising God for his goodness. There was a shout of joy by everyone and they danced and celebrated.

Manni told Lamarra, "I owe you four more days of your wedding week. We had three in Sychar."

She replied, "One day with you is a thousand, my love." Suddenly the music changed, and everyone looked to see what was next. A small figure was wrapped in a purple fabric on the floor. As the music played, the figure sat up and sprung forth to stand, it was Ilani! She began to twirl and

---

[99] Proverbs 31:10
[100] Mark 10:8

spin and dance for her parents. She was wearing her finger cymbals and was dancing wrapped in the purple shawl. She flipped and twirled. Manni and Lamarra didn't know she could dance so well! Suddenly she turned and looked over her shoulder and gave them the look!

Manni said, "Help me, lord!"

Lamarra laughed and agreed. "Help us Lord what are we going to do with her!" She continued to dance and twirled over to Samuel who was sitting with her cousins and gave him the look over her shoulders and he was hooked!!! His mouth hung open and all he could do was to stare at Ilani's beautiful eyes. She flipped her head and collapsed on the floor. Everyone stood and applauded. When she got up and bowed to her audience, Samuel was still in a state of shock.

She just laughed at him and gave her parents the biggest hug and said, "I love you, abba and mama."

They replied, "We love you, baby."

Manni said", Lamarra, what am I going to do with that girl?"

She said, "I don't know, but you better think fast because another child is coming in the spring!"

Manni looked at her, his mouth hung open "...what.... you're with child?" He grabbed her and hugged and kissed her and the crowd cheered and encouraged them more. Manni was crying with joy!

Lamarra said, "I had a dream that there were children all around me, and there were two little boys that looked just like you, sitting at my feet."

He said, "Oh my GOD!!!! Twins!"

"A double blessing," Lamarra said. She told him how before her father died, he anointed her and prayed over her and decreed a blessing over her. He prophesied to the sons in her womb that he did not hold in his arms, but he held up in his prayer. Manni kissed her and the crowd shouted for them even the more.

He said, "This is wonderful, you're with twins and Sarah is having their baby too. We all are so blessed!" They were so happy. As the night went on, the old widow came over to Manni and said,

"My son, the lord has given me a new purpose."

He said, "What is that, mother?"

She said, "He has shown me three children that I am to take care of and I offer myself as a nurse to your children and to any of your workers that may need my help. Will you build me a small house out of the way, where I can be of service to you?"

He said, "Mother, I will do no such thing!" She looked offended. He said, "If there will be any building it will be a room onto our home for you to live right here with us! You took my wife into your house when she was in need and now we need you to help us! Mother, you will live with your daughter and your son." She praised the lord and kissed her new son and thanked her new daughter. The Lord had prospered Manni and Lamarra and anyone who had blessed them, or they blessed. It was a joyful time for all, and they all received the blessings of the Lord, which made them rich and added no sorrow with it[101].

---

[101] Proverbs 10:22

For God so loved the world, that he gave his only begotten Son, that whosoever believeth in him should not perish, but have everlasting life. For God sent not his Son into the world to condemn the world; but that the world through him might be saved.

John 3:16-17 KJV

IN LOVING MEMORY AND TRIBUTE TO
MY HUSBAND,
PASTOR ORVIN L. TURNER

CPSIA information can be obtained
at www.ICGtesting.com
Printed in the USA
FFOW02n0251310118
44797014-44921FF